Fool on the Loch

Jack Kirk

FIDDIN - GREENOCK

Copyright 2016 by the Author

ISBN-13: 978-1537772608

ISBN-10: 1537772600

Introduction

The bright morning sun cut over the dark barrier of the Lomond hills illuminating peak after peak, some tipped with winter white even though summer was but a breath away. Loch after loch it lit leaving trailing fronds of gold thinly coating the water, shadows hiding rocky shores but leaving little dark islands on the gold blanket of water. Most were of treetops poking their way up from rocky island outcrops but, as the mist thinned it could be seen that one was of grey metallic grids and masts jarring with the soft surrounds.

The mist seemed to gather itself around this foreign isle, desperately trying to hide its ugliness from the light of day, but the sun eventually burned away the mist and the ugly shapes could be seen from afar.

There were very few who that day, or any other day, wished to see those shapes on that loch, or any other loch, but to some it was home, temporary that is, but home never the less, and one of those unfortunates at that moment lay plagued by the terrors of nightmared sleep!

Chapter 1

They were swarming up the sides of his ship, hundreds of them! Dishevelled harridans, waving gaudy banners touting the weird logo of "The Mothers against Polaris". And they were stripping off! Casting aside their ragged clothes and below they were dressed as --- Red Army soldiers! And the banners were turning to machine guns! Alarm bells were ringing, ringing, ringing!

Commander Barnaby Lewis Clarke woke up screaming, his telephone ringing harshly at the side of his bunk. He grasped it fiercely in his clammy nightmare sweated hand and gurgled incoherently into the receiver. The slow drawl of Gil Maitland jnr. seaman first class, came through the line.

'Good morning, Commander, its six twenty-five and you're comin' alive!'

'Like hell I am!' cursed the Commander. 'Now what the hell are you calling me for at this unearthly time of the morning?'

'Just like you instructed, sir.' replied the seaman. 'Your trawler friend just passed the point and is headed across the river to Greenock. A bit on the early side this morning but the same routine otherwise.'

The Commander gritted his teeth. 'Okay. Fine. Sorry about that. Keep a good lookout and let me know when he comes back on station.'

'Sure thing, Commander,' the seaman snapped. 'The Free World depends on our vigilance!'

The telephone clicked off. Lewis Clarke stared at it briefly. Did he, or did he not, detect a hint of sarcasm in that damn Alabaman's voice? Nobody really took the Commander seriously these days! He pulled himself together. Despite their scepticism he would save them from the commies! The Commander dialled the internal switchboard of the USS Bayou Leaf, support ship of the U.S. Navy submarine base at Loch Garnock in Scotland.

'This is Commander Local Security, gimme an outside line!'

'Sure, sir,' came the casual reply. 'Say, Commander, what's tonight's movie?'

Lewis Clarke swore silently. No wonder he wasn't taken seriously. "Local Security" was lumped in with the titles of Entertainments Officer, Food Inspection and Hygiene Officer, Welfare Officer, and worst of all, Liaison Officer to "The Mothers against Polaris."! Every shit detail added to his legitimate job, and most of that chipped away by those goons ashore in the C.I.A. But he would show them yet, not one of them had spotted that spy trawler yet!

'It's on the goddamn board!' he yelled in reply to the operator's enquiry. 'That's if you have enough sense to be able to read it! Now gimme that outside line!'

The commander cringed as he realised what he had just said. Senior officers did not lower their dignity to abusing junior seamen, but at times he just couldn't help himself, especially when he had moments before been fighting off a Russian invasion. In his dreams, that is. He could hear the seaman catch a breath then the click, click of him going through the motions. No doubt thinking about how he would be telling this story in the crew's mess at breakfast that morning.

'Okay, okay sir.' the seaman eventually said. 'I guess it's early all round, putting you through right now.'

Lewis Clarke pressed the now lit up red button for outside lines, dialled again and waited through the soft burr of the telephone at the other end.. A sleepy American voice finally answered.

'Seaman Padowski!' barked the Commander. 'Get down to the quay! Your subject's running early!'

'But sir,' the sleepy voice answered. 'It's only six-thirty!'

'Damn it sailor, get your fat butt moving! He'll be there in fifteen minutes!'

A soft sultry voice in the background made him blush slightly then he snarled in anger. 'Leave that floozy of your right now and get down there! Or else!'

He slammed the phone down and tried to compose himself. Surrounded by time servers and incompetents! He thought, and then tucked himself self righteously back into bed to catch another hour's sleep.

Some miles away a small launch lay in the glass like waters of Loch Fiddin where the mist had cleared and hardly a breath of wind ruffled the loch surface. Mirrored in these waters a solitary figure reeled in his fishing line and found a small fish twisting on the hook. Skilfully landed the fish was carefully measured; an educated estimate made of its weight, then unhooked and plopped among a few of its cousins in the catcher's creel. The measured results were studiously entered into a dog-eared notebook.

Colin Cameron, chief engineer of the bulk cargo ship "Farnhead", was enjoying another morning's fishing at his favourite spot near the shallow head of the loch where the River Fiddin entered the salt waters. His ship lay half a mile down the loch, looking vast and shiny in the early morning dew, seeming to float above the water surface on the wisps of mist still lingering around it. She had tarried there for some six months, laid up and loadless, a victim of the recession and vagrancies of the world shipping market.

To the chief engineer this was fine, not that he would mention that to the company's shareholders whose profits were tumbling, but to him sitting here in the loch close to where he called home, it was more than fine. He was getting paid the same rate as he would have been storming round Cape Horn or, even worse, laid up in some sweltering creek in Borneo, and at the same time, just over the hills lay his home and family who he could easily visit for a few nights at a time. For the rest of the time, apart from the occasional inspection of the ship along with the other few men tasked with looking after it, there was the loch and the fishing. Smiling to himself he checked the time, laid his rod aside, and opened up the small hamper he thought he had packed the previous night.

The haddock's head, eyes staring accusingly, stared up at Colin from the sandwich box, open mouth filled with a hardboiled egg still in its shell, a note pinned to its hard stiff lower lip.

'Those bloody twins!' murmured Colin with a grin. At least the sandwiches were still okay, packed in shrink wrap, safe from the fishy smell.

He read the note. 'Happy Birthday. Michael David and David Michael. Enjoy the rum.'

Rum? Thought Colin, quickly picking up his thermos flask and unscrewing the cup and the cap. He hungrily breathed in the hot sweet aroma of coffee laced sturdily with dark Barbados rum.

'Bloody beautiful twins!' he laughed out loud. 'They've found another bottle of the stuff!'

He settled back in the boat and poured himself a cup of the strong black liquid, bit into a sandwich and contemplated the loch, the hills, and the world in general. It was a fine day for contemplation, of the past, the present, and the future, or for whatever took a man's fancy on a morning like this. It was thirty years that month since he had gone to sea, first five hard years on his father's fishing boats, then ten wild years chasing around the world excited by the prospects of exotic ports and exotic women. Then he got married to the lass back home and the novelty of travelling wore off after the bairns arrived, and now he was thinking about moving ashore. In the meantime though he was quite content with this job to last a few months longer where he could sit about the loch where nothing changed and nothing disturbed his peace and solitude.

He finished the coffee, packed away his hamper after consigning the haddock head to the deep, and picked up his rod for the last few casts of the morning.

High on a hillside above the loch a disgruntled wet and cold officer of Her Majesty's Customs and Excise wished he had the foresight of the lone fisherman in the launch. The core of a hastily snatched and long consumed apple lay browning beside an empty coke can on the damp hillside. A chilled and bilious stomach belched bravely then settled down to a slow rumble as the man cursed quietly. 'Damn the super!' he muttered to nobody in particular except a nearby sheep which stared his way for a second before continuing to root at some straggly grass. 'And damn his bloody obsession with this loch! And double damn all bloody drug smugglers who keep an honest man out of bed at night!'

Jimmy Thomson's arms ached from the weight of the heavy night glasses which he refocused on the opposite shore. Momentarily distracted by the movements and the slight sound of unexpected laughter of the figure in the boat, he returned to his vigil. Only fifteen more minutes watching the white walls of the big house on the opposite shore which stood out clearly now against the dark hillside and he could go home. Still not a sign of life though after lying sitting or lying there for more than seven hours but maybe, he thought as a light went on in one attic window, he might get a flash of that pretty little maid getting dressed for the day. He just missed her undressing near midnight he had been told by the man he had relieved. All in the line of duty, of course! He decided though he would wait out another fifteen minutes before heading down to the village where his car was parked.

The village of Fiddin, only three miles across the River Clyde from the bustling town of Greenock, was a gem of antiquity set in the green hillsides of the Cowan Peninsula. Only by sea was it readily accessible until in a burst of misplaced generosity the far away central government of the day pushed a road down the west side of Loch Garnock, round the rocky point of Gowan and two miles up the east side of Loch Fiddin into the village, there stopped by the ever increasing slopes of the loch shore which became vertical not far beyond the village. At the same time they constructed a ferry slipway near Cowan point intending this to be the start of a major alternative tourist route to the Western Highlands of Scotland. Unfortunately, so the story goes, the map the politicians used only took in the peninsula and the north of it and went no further south. If it had it might have shown the long shelves of the Garnock rocks which made a very effective barrier to the new ferry slip!

Governments come and go and that government went shortly after the slip was completed, but the rocks remained, preventing all but the smallest ferries from approaching their new tourist terminal.

Fiddin slept on, practically undisturbed, for at only four cars per trip the tourists seldom used the new route. This tiny ferry had continued for thirty years as the only one to ply the route and though the local people used the ferry and were quite happy with it, few else ever did after trying it once. A lot of that had to do with the ever increasing age and unreliability of both its engines, and the eccentricities of its captain/owner, who also had admittedly a well deserved reputation for unreliability.

Still, it ran fairly in time with the local buses which, starting at Fiddin, struggled noisily round to the ferry landing, carried on round Loch Garnock past the American Navy submarine base pier and terminated at Helensburgh railway station some twenty odd miles and a few hair raising bends and hills away. Neither ferry nor bus ever really ran on time, but, by some clannish telepathy, as there were no phone communications, nearly always coincided at the ferry slip. Perhaps because the ferry skipper's younger brothers were the owners/operators of the two ancient buses which had struggled round the lochs for as long as the ferry had run, or perhaps it was just one more of the mysteries of the Highlands. Whatever, the unreliable but ever present system continued and some said that it had nothing to do with the brothers. Some said that the ferry and the buses were now so used to the ritual that they could carry on forever without the benefit of human intervention, but that may have been over-fanciful.

Regardless of the method though, it suited the hundred or so inhabitants of Fiddin just fine. Undisturbed by the tourist trade which normally used the upriver Erskine Bridge or the larger ferries further west, they fairly slumbered through the twentieth century. One pub, one shop, one small stone church and a few dozen whitewashed stone built houses; it seldom saw visitors and just as seldom wanted them. A little farming, a little fishing, and a quiet life was all that most people wanted, and who is to say that this was not the ideal life?

Colin Cameron tied up his boat at the village quay and

picked his way through the tangle of lobster creels and drying fishing nets, a few old fishermen giving him a brief greeting as he passed. Known more for his early years on fishing boats than for his present position as chief engineer on the laid up metal hulk lying in the loch, he was almost accepted by the locals as one of their own. Almost, he thought to himself, but never totally, not even if his ship sat there for the next ninety-nine years. Small villages are like that.

The local store was open, selling big brown rolls, locally baked and still warm at this early hour. The milk was brought in by Donald the dairyman whose real name was Anthony, but who would never have answered to it even if his life depended on it, and the Scottish and national newspapers were brought in by the first bus of the morning which surprisingly enough arrived very early in the morning and on time, though seldom managed to repeat that mistake at any other time of the day. With radio available and television reception, sometimes a bit patchy but mostly good, Fiddin was virtually a hub of civilisation. At least until winter came, and the roads were blocked by snow and as often as not the television and radio transmitters and receivers brought down by howling hilltop winds.

But it was a fine summery morning now, the day starting off with a smile on its face.

Jenny Dugan, eighteen years old and a dark haired Celtic beauty whose parents owned the local store, was serving the minister's wife with rolls and milk when Colin entered. No newspapers, of course, except the churches own weekly tome of gloom and perdition, ever found its way up the hill to the manse. "Lie sheets of those southern heathen devils!" the mistress of the manse was often and loudly heard to call the popular press, and many a poor soul who had been caught reading one of these newspapers was left in no doubt what fate awaited them come the day of judgement. Her husband though was a milder and more pleasant man and had to slip down later in the day, "in the course of his parish duties", borrow a paper from the local publican and slip into the back room of the Londoners Arms for a quiet read and a wee dram.

'I have to check what the heathen devils are up to before I know how to combat them.' he told everyone. Except his wife, of course, as he to liked a quiet life.

Colin always erred on the side of caution and left the newspapers alone until the minister's wife left as he saw no point in wasting his morning, but it did him little good as he still usually got a glare as she left. He had travelled to foreign parts, so must have been a sinner of some kind, even if unproven.

That morning as she turned away from the counter, her face reminded him of some of the pouting fish he had just caught, but he still, out of politeness, greeted her.

'Good morning, Mrs MacIver. I hope you and your husband are well.'

'It is a morning you would be doing well to praise the Lord for!' she retorted sternly.

'Oh, I do,' Colin said cheerfully. 'I've praised him six times already this morning for the six fine fish he's allowed me.'

Jenny Dugan gave a small giggle and in return earned a murderous stare from the un-amused minister's wife who then turned back on Colin.

'You should not be so flippant, Colin Cameron, for a man who earns his living on the seas stands very close to the fury of the storm. Only the Lord will protect you from that!'

Colin almost wished he had kept his mouth shut but was determined not to back down. He wasn't all that religious anyhow few people in his occupation were, and certainly he had not a great deal of respect for fanatics of any kind. 'I'm not being flippant.' Mrs MacIver.' he replied with a stern look. 'I'm just highly pleased, and I'm sure the Lord can't be too displeased with an old sinner like myself or he would not be so generous with his fish!'

Mrs MacIver stared stonily at him for a few moments, then stormed out clutching her rolls and milk to her offended bosom. Only when the door was safely shut did young Jenny burst out into open laughter, clapping her hands with glee and chalking up an imaginary score on an equally imaginary scoreboard. Colin smiled easily at her and approached the counter with a brisk step.

Jenny gave him a smile which was like the sun coming up. 'It's lovely to see you this morning, Mr Cameron, especially when you chase away the only cloud hovering above the village!'

Colin safely picked up several different newspapers and plumped them down on the counter in front of the smiling girl. 'Ach, Jenny, surely a little ray of sunshine like yourself should be able to cope with an old storm cloud like that?'

Jenny blushed slightly at the compliment and shook her head. 'She is such a misery though, that woman, and her husband is such a fine wee man. That he should be afflicted with an old sourpuss like her! Now,' she continued. 'Would you be wanting your usual order of rolls and milk?'

'Yes please, Jenny. And give me a jar of your mother's home made marmalade, a carton of Regency cigarettes as well, and a plain sliced loaf.'

The girl nodded and busied herself towards the back of the shop making up a couple of bags of groceries, while Colin looked through the newspapers. The Times for the Old Man, though their Captain seldom sobered up enough to read it, the Glasgow Herald for Angelo the cook, who constantly searched it for sales of restaurant premises in Glasgow, Sun & Star for the twins, and the Daily Record for himself. A fine bundle of wickedness for the minister's wife to consider, and later they would be shared around with everyone aboard to alleviate the inevitable boredom of the crew of his laid up vessel.

The shop door bell tinkled and a weary and slightly dishevelled figure entered, caught Colin's eye, and then turned abruptly away, appearing to find an all consuming interest in a selection of women's magazines. Colin thought for a moment then spoke up.

'Mr Thomson, is it not? We met six months ago when the Farnhead was first laid up.'

The man turned, looking a bit flustered. 'Yes, yes, sorry. I didn't recognise you at first.'

'No doubt you've seen a hundred captains and chief engineers since then.' Colin replied. He reintroduced himself but did not press the conversation after seeing an anguished plea for silence in the man's face.

Jenny returned with the two big bags of rolls, bread and milk and handed them to Colin, who paid up, thanked her and left the shop. The customs officer hastily paid for a newspaper and hurried after Colin, catching up with him and drawing him aside.

'Sorry about that.' he apologised. 'But I'd rather not too many people about here knew I was with the Customs!'

Colin chuckled quietly. 'No doubt if I was a Customs man I wouldn't want too many people knowing about it either. Now by any chance would you be searching the hills for some free enterprise whisky stills?

Thomson gave a deep sigh. 'If it was only that! I could fair be doing with a wee dram, illegal or not!'

Colin shrugged. 'You'd be lucky to find the illegal stuff these days; it's a dying art, mores the pity. Used to be some nice stuff made around here in the old days. Well, if it's not that, what are you after? Fiddin is hardly the sort of place to attract any big time boys cheating on the Queen and country!'

Thomson looked around to ensure no other ears were listening. The fishermen were still chatting away along the quay, a couple of ancient locals stood leaning on a park bench staring across the loch at nothing particular, and two school-bagged children walked along the street towards the tiny village primary school. Reassured the customs man spoke up.

'I shouldn't really be telling you this, sir, but I take you for an honest and discreet man, Mr Cameron.'

Colin nodded in confidence.

'Well, you see sir; I'm part of a team looking for drug smugglers.'

Colin almost laughed and covered it up by giving a sort of surprised grunt. 'I doubt if you'll find too many up this loch. They are too fond of the whisky around here to be bothered with anything more modern.'

Thomson just shrugged. 'I know that, Mr Cameron, but we have an Englishman in charge and drug smugglers are an absolute obsession with him! I'm pretty sure we're wasting our time about here but I'd appreciate it if you didn't mention any of this. Excise men have never been too popular about these parts.'

Colin smiled. 'Or any other parts I'd bet!'

He saw the dismay in the young officer's face and hurried to assure him. 'Fair enough. But the lads on the ship will recognise you from the time the ship was laid up, though they know you were more than fair with them then, so I think I should let them know you are around but not to mention it to any of the locals when they are ashore in the pub or at the shop.'

Thomson screwed up his face. 'Aye, they would know me! For that matter that cook of yours knew me before

15

that when I pinched a couple of his shipmates in Greenock last year!'

'Oh aye.' Colin said. 'For what might I ask?'

The customs man looked a bit embarrassed and answered hesitatingly. 'Well, contraceptives from Brazil. Well, so called contraceptives as they wouldn't have kept a warm breeze in.'

Colin did laugh this time. 'Hardly a big deal!'

Thomson cringed. 'Four thousand packets at a fiver apiece? A lot of unwanted pregnancies, Mr Cameron!'

Colin nodded agreement. 'Well Angelo has six kids and is Catholic in descent so probably would agree with you on the arrest, so he'll keep quiet about it. The rest I'll make damn sure they don't shop you.'

'Just make sure you don't tell them about the drugs business.' Thomson said with a pleading look on his face. 'If that got about my boss might start to look over here, and I can assure you, you don't want that to happen.'

'True enough!' Colin exclaimed. 'We don't want any heavy footed Sassenachs wandering about disturbing the fishing!'

In agreement the two men continued along the short street, Thomson to his car and Colin to his boat. They passed the two ancients at the bench in silence and were barely out of earshot before one of them turned to the other.

'Here Calum, who is that went bye with young Colin Cameron?'

'Och Willie, your sight is really getting bad! That was young Jimmy Thomson from Greenock. You will be knowing his father and grandfather as well. The whole family have been bliddy revenue men for generations!'

'Ah,' Willie nodded in agreement. 'That's the one Gregor was telling me about earlier. Him that's been hanging about up on the crags watching the loch with his big binoculars.'

'That's right; Gregor was in a wee bit of a panic at first, seeing as he nearly fell over his wee still just as the mash was reaching a critical point! Could have ruined a complete batch of the whisky, but luckily he never even noticed it! Too intent in looking across the loch at god knows what.'

'Ach well, as long as God keeps him looking in that direction we should get a good few nips out Gregor's latest batch.' The man licked his lips, remembering the last batch of illegal whisky produced up the hill above the village. 'God really does work in mysterious ways!'

Colin and the customs man shook hands and were about to part ways when Colin remembered his fish. 'By the way, would you like a couple of sea trout? I'd a fair catch this morning and the lads are getting fed up with me filling the fridge up with fish.'

Jimmy Thomson brightened up. 'Thanks very much, sir. I'm fairly partial to fresh sea trout.'

Colin got a couple out and loosely wrapped them with a bit of old cellophane from the pocket of his bag. 'Maybe you could give one to that boss of yours. It will give him something even if he finds nothing else here.'

'Give him fresh sea trout!' Jimmy exclaimed. 'I wouldn't waste it on him! The damn Sassenach still thinks that fish are caught with bread-crumbed fingers on them!'

Chapter 2

The "damn Sassenach" in question was shortly afterwards storming into his office up a rather scruffy alley in the damp and dreary port of Greenock. Already highly unhappy over his posting to these northern parts of the British Isles it had not improved his disposition that morning when he awoke to find his car, all four tyres let down and a St Andrews cross spray painted on the bonnet. Very artistically painted to be sure, but helping not one bit to get the tyres pumped up.

Cecil Smythe Smith suspected a family down the street from his rented flat for this disgraceful sabotage of the official transport of a senior member of HM Customs and Excise. All four sons in the family being patriotic Scotsmen and also British Merchant Navy seamen, a breed not especially known for its love of the Customs service, they were his prime suspects. He suspected though it could have been any one of the thousands of people in Greenock. None of them liked an Englishman let alone a Customs officer in their midst. The previous week Smythe Smith was convinced though that members of the same family had been super-gluing shut the car's doors, but knowing and proving were different matters. The local police had not been all that sympathetic. 'Consider yourself lucky you were not in it at the time.' a police sergeant had said. 'Then they would have probably set it on fire as well!'

This did not help his frustration at the present attacks on him and he was in a bad mood as he entered the office.

'A bit late you are this morning, superintendent.' stated

a ruddy faced Scotsman from a corner desk crowded with a largely ignored pile of paper. The man's dress, totally at odds with his present environment, consisted of a black knitted cap, Fair Isle jersey, corduroy trousers and fisherman's boots, but neverless he normally went by the title of Sergeant Donald Donaldson and was the local expert and liaison man between the police and the customs squad, and was prepared for another day at trying to be incognito.

'A bloody disgrace!' screamed Smythe Smith, launching into a detailed description of that mornings indignity. 'Get onto your local colleagues about it, sergeant! I am not having my operations sabotaged by a bunch of drunken seamen!'

'Now superintendent, I doubt if it's really a malicious act, just the boys' way of celebrating our victory over the Germans.'

Smythe Smith gave him a puzzled look. 'Victory? Germans? We beat those blighters forty years ago! They can't still be celebrating the end of the war!'

'The football match, sir.' the sergeant patiently explained. 'Last night Scotland beat East Germany three goals to nil. It was a great victory to get in an away match, you must admit.'

'I'll admit nothing of the kind!' shouted the indignant customs chief. 'I'm not running this operation to suit a bloody game! I can't afford to lose half a morning every time some idiot kicks a ball into the back of a net and some other idiots consider that to be of some importance!'

The sergeant sighed deeply, more in pity than anger. 'I suppose you're right, sir, but I don't think you should be saying anything like that if you happen to be standing in a local pub. It's as likely you would be missing a lot more than half your teeth the next morning!'

Smythe Smith thought about that for a few moments

then grunted. He shuffled some paperwork on his desk then abruptly changed the subject.

'Has Thomson phoned in yet?'

'About half an hour ago. He called from the public phone in Fiddin. He'll be catching the local ferry about now and should be in the office within the hour.'

'And what happened?'

'Nothing at all, sir.' replied the sergeant. 'It is just as I thought, he will find nothing amiss in Fiddin House. I know Sir John Cohen fairly well and he's a decent man who has done a lot for the area.'

'A bloody wartime black marketer!' retorted Smythe Smith angrily. 'Where do you think he got the money for that bloody mansion, and all his flunkeys, and that big yacht he sails about in, and I've no doubt he uses it to smuggle drugs!'

The sergeant frowned, a bit angrily this time, and felt he had to defend a man who he had some respect for. 'Now super, maybe he did do a wee bit of dubious trading back in the old days, but then, so did half the present government and a few of the Lords and Ladies in the upper house. No more than them, does that make them drug smugglers! Besides, from what we found through Interpol, that yacht of his has never left its berth in Monte Carlo for more than a couple of days in the last two years! It's no Concorde, you know!'

'Neither here nor there!' Smythe Smith fired back. 'A man with his sort of money could buy half a dozen yachts which we know nothing about!'

The sergeant shook his head. 'I would have thought, sir, with all that money, he would not have been happy to risk it by doing a bit of smuggling.'

The Customs man scowled at that. 'We will see, sergeant, we will see. I've got a hunch about this one!'

Smythe Smith settled his plump middle age figure into

a protesting metal framed chair and indicated the conversation was closed. 'Now where's today's mail.'

The sergeant pointed at the pile of paper on his bosses desk which the owner had shuffled over the mail a moment before and studiously began examining some of his own paperwork, most of which dealt with nothing but rumours and hunches and would be in the bin before the end of the day.

The mail was disposed off in a different manner, Smythe Smith never threw anything away, and what was not pushed over to the sergeant's desk was carefully filed away to gather dust. Not that there was a lot of that. Little official seemed to reach this far north anyhow, the Customs man thought. Not as much as an acknowledgment of his copious reports diligently sent to his superiors in London. Not even a reply to his request for better and bigger offices. They had though sent a reply to his request for another filing cabinet, turning it down flat! He silently fumed over his banishment to these northern isles to set up a so called secret unit independent of the main Customs and Excise service, wondering if this was simply to move an overzealous officer away into the wilds, but dismissed the idea immediately. He was far too valuable a man for that! Smythe Smith though did suspect that as far as the service was concerned, Hadrian's Wall still blocked the border.

The office door swung open and a bearded grizzled figure rolled in, his fisherman's garb even more despicable than the sergeants, but in this case it was the man's normal working clothes and nothing to do with a part he was playing.

'Fine day for the loch, is it not, Donald?' he asked the sergeant, then turned to the Customs man. 'And how is yourself, super-inten-dent?'

The West Highland voice dragged out Smythe Smith's

rank till it almost sounded like an insult, though Hector Donaldson had no deliberate intent. He considered that being English was a big enough burden to carry without insulting a customs officer any further.

The man in question grunted a non-committal reply and went back to his solitary fuming, not even noticing the unmeant insult.

'Good Morning yourself.' the sergeant answered with a shrug, a shake of his head, and with easy familiarity, for apart from being cousins, in the past two weeks Hector and his boat had been hired to help out in some of their more clandestine activities.

The sergeant turned to his boss. 'Would you be wanting us to watch the same place today?'

'Of course!' Smith exclaimed, shaking himself out of his sulk. 'We can't let up our vigilance for a moment or the blighters will flood the country with drugs!'

The sergeant doubted that a lot of drugs would be coming in past them that day but going out on the boat would keep him well away from this morose Englishman. Besides, it would also maybe give him a chance to do a little fishing. He rose and picked up a duffle bag and went to leave.

'And I want your reports typewritten after this.' added his boss. 'I can hardly read your writing!'

The sergeant gave another quiet nod but Hector let out a loud and disgusted snort. 'And you will no doubt be wanting a secretaries office built into my wee boat as well? With a coffee machine and some filing cabinets?'

The sergeant hustled Hector out the door before the superintendent could reply; knowing fine that the very mention of filing cabinet would really send the super into a tirade that could really ruin their day just it had ruined the super's.

As the two cousins wound their way through the back streets of Greenock, Donald wondered how much longer he would enjoy the idyllic life, sitting up Lock Garnock every day watching the American liberty men going ashore from the nuclear submarine tender. For over a week now he and Hector had kept their vigil with no signs of an emerging pattern in the seamen's movements. Still, it was better than being stuck in that tiny office with an English revenue man!

Neither cousin noticed the furtive figure of Elton Padowski lurking in a convenient alley as they passed, then start after them as they made there way down to where Hector's boat was berthed. The American seaman enjoyed playing sleuth, even though he resented being dragged from a warm and friendly bed at an early hour. He had little choice though, Commander Clarke had made it very clear, no detective work, no nightly passes to Greenock, and no more fun filled nights with "Hot Helen", his local comfort and love. He shivered in anticipation of that night's probable frolics and hurried after the two men, dodging among the increasing crowds of shipyard and dock workers in an effort at concealment.

Hector's boat, the Dhu Mohr, was a typical small west coast fishing boat, wooden hulled and squat with a small square wheelhouse, it drew no attention in the small inshot of the harbour where half a dozen close relatives of it ran out most days to do inshore fishing. Not a lot of money in that trade though for it, nor any others, including those from its home port of Fiddin, only the windfall of the customs charter had paid off a few debts and saved the boat from the final indignity of seizure by the banks or more likely the scrapheap! Few boats had escaped one or the other of these, and fewer still now sailed from the Clyde to chase the shoals of herring, though some of lately had taken to chasing oil rigs as an alternative way of earning a living.

So now few fishermen were left to crowd the quay, far too few for a stranger not to be noticed, and the average crew-cutted American was likely to stand out like a hamburger at a haggis party, so Padowski slipped behind a convenient shed until the cousins boarded the boat and cast off. The Dhu Mohr slowly chugged clear of the harbour, its single cylinder Ailsa engine sending smoke signals into the clear morning air, then Padowski strolled along the quay to question a casual lounger whose sole interest seemed to be some distant point in a completely empty patch of sky.

'Fine boat that.' Padowski said pointing to the departing Dhu Mohr.

'Seen better.' stated the lounger, hardly even twitching except for his lips.

'You know who owns it?' Padowski persisted.

'Do that.' replied the man, still appearing to be engrossed in the empty patch of sky.

Padowski followed his gaze and saw absolutely nothing, not even a seagull, not even a cloud. Goddamn weird Jocks, he thought to himself, then continued his attempt at interrogation.

'So who owns it?'

The man finally left his vigil of the heavens and turned to Padowski. 'And who would it be that wants to know?'

'Well---I'm, -- I might be interested in buying it.'

'I see.' said the man, though it was obvious that he didn't and this excuse was something of a strain on his credibility. 'I suppose you might just be daft enough!' He then gave a disinterested shrug. 'It's no skin off my nose though. It belongs to Hector Donaldson of Fiddin and maybe, just maybe, he might be interested in selling it.'

The man appeared to consider the conversation closed and went back to studying the vacant sky, moving his head around a bit as if he wanted to focus on exactly the same place as before.

Padowski couldn't help but look again and again found nothing there. He snapped his gaze away and tried to engage the man in conversation again. 'You don't happen to know the name of the man who was with him?' he asked.

'With who?' asked the lounger, without moving his head a millimetre.

Padowski screwed up his face but persisted. 'This guy Hector Donaldson.'

The man gave a long resigned sigh and turned slightly towards the American sailor. 'You've an awful lot of questions you Americans but, if it will help dispel your ignorance I suppose I should answer you as precisely as possible. The fact is, I don't really know!'

Padowski nearly exploded but held onto his frustration as the man continued.

'He has a familiar look to him, to be sure, but somehow different. Maybe you should be asking Hector himself.'

He gave Padowski a long hard look. 'When you ask him about buying the boat, that is!'

Padowski had a feeling he and his country had just been insulted but the man had turned away again and was again studying the sky. Also a couple of other big rough looking men in fishermen's clothes were wandering over looking for something to break up their boredom, or maybe break up Padowski to have something to do. 'Maybe I just will.' Padowski muttered more to himself than his reluctant informant. 'Maybe I'll just do that.'

He hurried off to catch the Fiddin ferry before any damage was done to him, and would be only be happy when he was across the river and onto the bus that would take him along past the submarine base.

Aboard the fifty thousand ton bulk cargo ship Farnhead, Colin Cameron strolled up the deck towards the forecastle. The sun warmed the steel and the smell of fresh paint hung in the air, and two boiler-suited figures armed with large paint rollers methodically spread thick red paint across the plating. Their movements were near identical; a rhythm that was both efficient and relaxed, and apart from different paint patches, the clothing was the same. And the carrot hair and cheery faces beneath matched exactly.

Colin had long since stopped trying to separate the twins. David Michael and Michael David Jones, forty-four years between the two of them, and as full of mischief as forty-four monkeys, but first class workers none the less. Officially they were respectively third mate and fourth engineer of the vessel, but in lay-up conditions it mattered little and Colin worked them both as one and generally got the work of three out of them.

'Morning, Chief!' they chorused cheerfully, then stepped quickly aside.

Across the deck, skilfully written in three foot high red letters, was the message "Happy Birthday" written in a flowery script.

Colin laughed and shook his head. 'Good morning to you, boys, and thanks for the wee surprise in my coffee this morning. And I believe the seagulls enjoyed the haddock's head as well!'

The twins grinned. 'How do you like the painting?' they asked simultaneously.

'Very artistic, I'm sure, but maybe you had better get it covered up before the old man looks out his window and sees it.'

The right hand twin scoffed. 'He'd be lucky to see it even if it was forty feet high and painted on his cabin bulkhead!'

'Mind you,' the left hand twin continued, 'If it was an

eighth of an inch high and printed on the label of a whisky bottle, he would probably spot it from four hundred yards in dense fog!'

Colin shook a cautionary finger at the speaker. 'Don't talk ill of your superior officers,' he scolded, though he knew full well it was probably true. 'Some day you might be captain yourself and just as fond of a few drinks to relax.'

'Not me.' answered the twin who had last spoken, as he turned and pointed at his brother. 'He'll be the boozy Old Man and I'll be the stone cold sober Chief Engineer!'

'Aye, I'll believe that about the sober bit.' Colin scoffed, but pointed at the youth. 'Anyhow, then it's you I want today!

It was a minor triumph to get the twins to admit who was who and especially when the job was not all that pleasant. He indicated the forward end of the vessel. 'Come on then, Michael David, it's time we did an inspection of the duct keel!'

The one twin laughed and the other shrugged and they all headed forward, as such an inspection could only be safely done by at least three men, the third not entering the space, but instead staying at the top to ensure they got out the other end safely. Running some six hundred feet from near the bow to the forward end of the engine room the duct keel burrowed beneath the massive cargo holds flanked by ballast and fuel tanks and was two interlinked side by side tunnels, one almost filled by torturous sinews of steam, fuel, bilge, compressed air and ballast lines, the other almost clear. It was barely five foot high but punctuated every three feet or so by leg stretching cross frames a foot and a half high at least and more at every fourth frame. Just to make life awkward each frame had its counterpart hanging down from the hold deck above, all giving minimum accessibility and maximum possibility of concussion.

In the art of obstruction naval architects had reached their ultimate in the design of these spaces, and every seaman who had to traverse this obstacle course agreed on one thing. All naval architects deserved keel hauling!

They kitted out in the forecastle with equipment already there, a strong belt to hang a few tools, a large flashlight, and bag containing half a dozen light bulbs, heavy leather gloves and hard hats. Well Michael David did but Colin instead pulled on a thick leather skipped cap that looked like it had come out of Noah's ark and caused both the twins to grin. It was hardly standard safety equipment but if there was ever anything Colin detested it was the hard hats supplied by the company.

'Did you get that from your great grandfather?' David Michael asked cheekily?'

Colin gave the youth a warning look. 'If some day you near hang yourself from a pipe bracket when the skip of your hard hat catches on it and pulls the strap backwards over your throat, you will wish your great grandfather had been as generous as well!'

The twin shrugged. 'You know best Chief.' He conceded. 'But if a forty foot container drops on your head maybe that hat won't do you a lot of good.'

Colin shook his head. 'If a forty footer drops on a hard hat all it will be good for is scooping up the mess it makes!'

Finished dressing, Colin opened up the door leading down to a small forward pump room and made sure the ventilation fans he had put on earlier were running and the lights were on. 'Call the bridge and let them know we're going in.' he told the third mate twin.

As the one twin complied and got word back on the radio, the other started down the very steep zigzag ladders that led down. Colin followed a bit slower letting the younger man move on ahead, where at the bottom he could open up the dogged down hatch leading the last six feet or so down into the duct keel. No sense employing a dog and barking yourself.

A few minutes later they started along the near empty side of the of twin set of tunnels, checking for anything at all out of the ordinary and listening for anything that could be construed as a leak of any fluid or air. The place was eerily silent and though there were overhead safety lights every ten feet or so it was most certainly creepy, the lights from the parallel tunnel especially casting weird shadows into theirs. It was not long before Michael picked up the vibes and had to say something.

'Somebody was up on the hillside again this morning, Chief, and appeared to be watching you.'

'And you were watching him, Michael?'

'Not so much, Chief, he was in a shadow, but I could see the movement as sometimes the sun caught the glass of his binoculars.'

Colin scraped his leg on a across a beam, the rust rough and scaly, and swore slightly causing the young engineer to turn round and catch the look on the Chief's face. 'You knew he was there?'

Colin stopped for a moment and decided this was as good a time as any. Getting one of the twins alone was so much easier than trying to deal with the quick fire returns of the two together. 'I met a customs man in Fiddin this morning.'

Michael looked at him quizzically. 'Not much for a customs man in the village, is there? We are about the only thing of interest around here!'

'Maybe he's looking for all that rum which you and your brother keep finding.' Colin half joked.

'Come off it, Chief! There's hardly more than a couple of bottles left anyhow and nobody outside the ship knows about it!'

'What about the man who hid it?' Colin asked.

'Patrick O'Hagan! He hid so much of the stuff before we laid up that he could never find the half of it! And even he is not stupid enough to shop himself to the customs.'

Colin ignored the implied insult to his fellow Chief Engineer. He didn't like O'Hagan much himself. 'Still Michael, he might be getting a wee bit annoyed that the pair of you can always find it when I'm doing my stint aboard and never a thing when he takes over.'

'Look Chief, he might be the man aboard here when you are off, but it doesn't mean to say I have to like him!'

'He's not that bad Michael, just a bit over boisterous at times. Works hard, plays hard.'

'It's not the working that bothers me, Chief; it's his idea of play! I'm not keen on people whose idea of fun is to spike my morning coffee with laxative!'

Colin attempted to stifle a small laugh but eventually gave forth. Michael David glared at him briefly, shrugged his disapproval away, and let his natural good humour take over again. Colin got himself under control and waved the youngster onwards till he got the last laugh out.

A moment later, the silence creeping up on him as well, he was glad when the boy turned briefly with a grin. 'It's just as well there are a lot of spare toilets aboard this ship.'

Colin laughed again. 'Well I hope you are fine this morning, Michael. It's a long way to the end of this tunnel and the nearest toilet!

The youngster acknowledged with a wave of his hand and they moved on, stopping a minute later when they came to a failed safety light. Colin held a torch on it as Michael unfastened the sealed glass, replaced the bulb and bolted the glass fitting back on.

Colin got his breath back in the interval and then spoke. 'Concerning this customs man. If you happen to see him about the village, just ignore him, and don't mention him to any of the villagers. If we leave the customs alone then they might do the same to us.'

Michael tightened up the light fitting nuts and nodded. 'Fair enough, but what's he up to?'

Colin gave him hard look. 'None of our business! I'm enjoying the quiet life and I'll be mightily displeased if you or your brother were the cause of any hassle!'

Michael shrugged and smiled. 'Anything you say, Chief. David and I are enjoying the quiet life here as well.' Then he gestured aft and started along the cold tomb of the duct keel. 'Even if you do drag us into this purgatory every couple of weeks.'

Colin followed then stopped dead. 'What do you mean, "us"? It's only you that comes down here.'

Michael turned and pointed his flashlight up at his face and grinned like some weird demon. 'Last time it was David who volunteered. He was trying very hard to keep out of the way of the Old Man that morning!'

Colin blew out his breath and waved the youth on. It hardly mattered in the end up who was with him as both the twins were competent enough to do the simple jobs required on these under hull trips and it done a third mate no harm to be down here, he probably had before as an apprentice. Still, it annoyed him that at work he still could not tell them apart!

'Well seeing you are so clever,' he called after Michael. 'See if you can find another bottle of O'Hagan's rum while you are down here!'

Michael grinned as he turned back. 'Already done Chief.' He held up a dark bottle. 'David spotted it the last time when you were in the other tunnel but couldn't reach it from there. I picked it up when you were busy tripping over that beam!'

Colin shook his head as the youth shoved the bottle back

in with the light bulbs and followed on behind him as his fine baritone voice echoed back along the tunnel happily singing a slightly rude version of "Island in the Sun" which rattled along the tunnel breaking off lumps of rust.

Had the pair not been incarcerated in the bowels of the ship they would certainly have heard the bellow from the lofty heights of the accommodation structure, a bellow that wafted out open doors and windows and echoed round the alleyways like the sound of Moby Dick's whale voice. David Michael, five hundred feet ahead even heard it, checked his watch, and carried on painting. Angelo Parnelli, the ship's diminutive cook also heard it, checked the clock on the bulkhead of the temporary little galley come pantry in which he spent most of his day, then lifted a tray containing one mug of steaming black coffee and headed up the one flight of stairs. Nine o'clock on the dot, and father had arisen and demanded his due. The Captain may have been a potential candidate for liver and kidney failure but he was very consistent in his habits. Twenty unbroken years of drinking and passing out and awakening at the same time made him near as accurate as the ship's expensive chronometer.

'Angelo! Where's my bloody coffee!' the captain roared as the cook almost stepped into the office, and a lesser man would have shrunk back spilling the coffee, but Angelo was quite used to by now. A portly bearded figure of fifty-eight years and a similar waist size in inches stood there in dishevelled shorts and stained Tee-shirt. His red grained eyes blearily looked at the cook and his unsteady rubbery legs weaved unsteadily towards a chair behind his desk.

'Good morning, Captain, Sir. Fine morning out, Sir.' Angelo said as he moved to open the curtains on the darkened room.

'Leave those bloody curtains alone!' bellowed the captain. 'Bloody sunshine gives me a headache in the morning.'

Angelo left them alone and deposited the coffee on the desk. 'Okay, Captain. What you want for lunch today, Sir?'

'Any damn thing you're cooking Angelo. What's O'Hagan having?'

'No idea, Captain. Mr O'Hagan is home on leave. Chief Engineer Mr Cameron on board.'

'Damn people keep changing here.' grumbled Captain Bernard Darwin, who found it a constant irritation that no matter how often changes were made he ended up the only Englishman aboard, and therefore, by his own estimation, the only civilized man among these primitive natives. 'What's Cameron having then?' he asked as he sipped his scalding tar like coffee.

The cook reeled of a lunch menu that would have shamed a five star hotel, which, for a few years was where Angelo had worked before wandering back to sea. Neither the superb cuisine nor excellent qualifications of the cook mattered to the captain. He had never made it down to lunch since the ship was laid up, seldom for dinner, and it was doubtful if he remembered what breakfast was. Nourishment consisted mainly of mounds of corned beef sandwiches washed down by copious quantities of Scotland's major liquor export.

'Fish again.' grumbled the captain, picking on one of the six possible dishes. 'Cameron's been out in the boat again, I take it?'

'Chiefy he fish good, I cook good. We all eat good.' the cook said sorrowfully as he looked at the captain. 'Captain, Sir, you come down for lunch today. Better than corned beef sandwiches for you. Much better when you drink a lot!'

'Drink a lot? Don't be silly, man, I hardly drink at all!' He looked vaguely towards the calendar on his desk, which was of little help, being the previous years. 'I take it the stores arrive today? I'm getting a trifle short of whisky.'

The cook sighed in resignation. He knew the captain would never change, but he liked to try occasionally.

'Stores not till tomorrow, Captain, but maybe I have one spare bottle. I bring it up later.'

'Before noon, Angelo, better before noon. I you see the Chief around tell him to come up for a peg.'

'Okay, Captain, I bring it up and tell Chiefy to come up.'

The cook left heading back downstairs to the pantry. Half an hour before I have to start lunch, thought the little cook, time to finish off another scarf. Reaching the pantry he stowed away the coffee tray and picked up his knitting needles and wool and continued to pursue his favourite pastime.

Chapter 3

The Dhu Mohr rounded Appan Point and headed up Loch Garnock towards the American submarine base, with Sergeant Donaldson enjoying the morning air as the small craft trundled across the sunny but choppy waters of the Clyde. As it moved into the more sheltered waters of the loch he stepped into the small wheelhouse to talk to his cousin.

'I wish you would not bait the superintendent so much, Hector. It just gets the Sassenach more annoyed and harder to work with.'

'I just can't help it, Donald.' the other replied with a shrug. 'The man is such a stuffed shirt! So full of himself and so full of bullshit!

The old fisherman hauled the engine throttle back at that point and put his wheel hard over to avoid an early morning yachtsman, missing the terrified man by little more than three very deliberate feet. 'Damn Wafi!' he roared at the amateur sailor, scaring him more but at the same time sending enough irate air towards him to puff out the man's sail and send him well clear.

Donald frowned at that shout and looked at his cousin. 'Just what is a "Wafi"?'

'Wind Assisted F---ing Idiot.' Hector said with a grin. 'I got that from one of the lads that works on the fast ferry to Belfast. It's what their captain calls them yachtie types!'

Donald smiled at that. Just showed you that even Hector could pick up some modern expressions, and then he put on his serious face again and continued his interrupted conversation. 'Hector, och, the poor superintendent was just a wee bit unfortunate in his last job, that is all, and it has maybe made him a wee bit bitter. So now he tries a wee bit too hard.'

'It makes it a wee bit hard on everybody about him a well!' Hector pointed out. 'Now don't get me wrong, Donald, I'm not complaining about the present situation. The fishing has been none to good this year and a few shillings extra, especially if they happen to be English government shillings, are always welcome.'

Donald shook his head. 'Ah well, Hector, I know you really have nothing against the man, except he is Customs, and he is English, and like the rest of us, he deserves as much pity for that as condemnation!'

Hector nodded and made another course alteration for no apparent reason other than he knew there was a rock forty feet under his boat and who knew when it might decide to pop up? The boat then cut diagonally across the loch towards the east shore and the landing used by the American liberty boats, keeping well clear of the dull gray hull of the base ship, the floating dry-dock and the attendant auxiliary vessels which made an untidy huddle in the middle of the loch. A sleek black shape was tucked against the base ship's side giving sinister purpose to the whole assembly and two purposeful looking launches sat protectively off it, the crews no doubt watching every move made by the Dhu Mohr and any other fishing boats making their way up towards the head of the loch.

'Like a pile of tin cans thrown in a puddle!' observed Hector with a contemptuous snort.

'Tin cans with big bangs!' retorted Donald. 'Just don't be going too close to them for they are always a bit jumpy and might just turn your wee wooden boat into a wee wooden pile of matchsticks!'

Hector swung the boat over to the short jetty adjoining a large car park almost filled with expensive transatlantic or continental cars. High wire fencing surrounded it leaving only a small gap at the jetty and a smaller at the road, it dominated by a sturdy gatehouse and blocked by a heavy steel wire gate. Several bored looking U.S. Marines stood behind the gate confronting a mob of wild chanting women.

'I see the dawn chorus is out again in force, this morning.' Hector said as he slowed the boat and manoeuvred it into position a hundred yards or so off the jetty.

'Damn nuisance, the lot of them!' growled the police sergeant as he stepped out onto the foredeck and picked up the hooked anchor stowed there. He continued in a purely unofficial manner. 'I would dearly love to get the whole lot of them with their scrawny necks round this rope!'

He heaved the small bow anchor over the side, watching the coil of anchor rope with satisfaction as it unwound rapidly into the depths of the loch. When it went slack he secured the rope and nodded to Hector who backed up the engine and waited till the rope again became firm and taut, then shut the engine down allowing the boat to swing securely. Then Hector joined his cousin on the foredeck.

'I heard you had a little trouble with them last month.' he said innocently.

The sergeant gave an annoyed grumble. 'A couple of my boys got a bit rough with them when we had to shift them off the road over there which they were blocking with their big fat behinds! The inspector, who is a foolish politically minded man, was not pleased at the way I handled it! But I could not let a bunch of daft women defy the law!'

He pointed across at the still chanting group of women. 'They can be a vicious nasty bunch themselves when they want to be! Kneed a couple of my lads in the family jewels which they did not take to at all!'

Hector laughed out loudly, his voice echoing over the loch and earning a curious look from a couple of sailors standing along the quay. 'Maybe they thought you policemen had a nuclear tipped missile stuck down their trousers!'

Donald grimaced back. 'Mothers against Polaris, be damned! I suspect more than a few of them never knew their fathers!'

The two men finished of securing the anchor, checked round the boat for loose ropes or any other problems, then settled down on a couple of battered old cushioned chairs to watch the American jetty. Smythe Smith had requested an accurate description of any serviceman going ashore with more than normal frequency hoping that this might lead to the discovery of a major smuggling operation. What would be considered normal neither man knew, so diligently, Donald and Hector had noted all movements along with simple descriptions such as "red haired six footer" and "short slim with wire glasses" and allocated them numbers. All this led to reams of paper crossing the customs inspector's desk where they were copied, filed, and more copies sent to London, where, as no answers were ever sent back, they were obviously ignored.

Sergeant Donaldson was himself quite sure that the whole exercise was futile in the extreme, but his was not to reason why. And it was a much more pleasant way of spending the brief time left before his retirement than being cooped up in an office with Smythe Smith, pushing piles of paperwork to and fro. The thought of that fate made him shudder, as did the thought of tangling with that wild female bunch safely a hundred or so yards away across deep water. He settled down with a benign smile and began counting American heads, but didn't get far before his talkative cousin disturbed his peace again.

'Do you think it was maybe your brush with those

harridans that got you stuck on this job with that daft Englishman?'

Donald shrugged. 'Could be, Hector, could very well be! I have the feeling that all of us in the squad are being punished for recent brushes with authority, for none of us have been told a damn thing about what we are really supposed to be doing here! And that includes the superintendent even though he pretends to know what's going on!'

'And what exactly did he do himself to be pushed away up here so far from the golden pavements of London?' enquired Hector sarcastically.

'You surely must have heard about the carry on at Heathrow Airport? It was even shown on the television news for a couple of days.'

'Television? Man, I only listen to the radio to get the fishing and weather reports.' scoffed Hector. 'I don't suppose I have even read a newspaper right through for months except maybe the Oban Times, and somehow I don't think they have too many reporters at that big sprawl of an airport!'

'Hector,' sighed the sergeant. 'You really should try to keep up with what goes on in the world.'

'And why should I want to be doing something like that? It is a fine life I have here with nobody much bothering me, so I see no point in complicating it or wasting my time by reading about other people's miseries. Nothing but sex and violence in the newspapers anyway, I mean, look at the goings on of that politician with his Mandy Potato and Christine Peeler. Why would I want to know the ins and outs of that lot?'

'It was Mandy Rice Davies and Christine Keeler.' Donald pointed out. 'And that was donkey's years ago. Still, I had a rare laugh when I saw that Heathrow carry on. No doubt though, that Smythe Smith was not doing much laughing the next day!'

'Let's be hearing what happened then. Donald, I could fine be doing with a good laugh, especially if it concerns that old sourpuss!'

The sergeant made himself a bit more comfortable on the chair, lit up his pipe, and began to recount his tale.

'The superintendent was a big man down at yon Heathrow Airport, in charge of the whole drug squad even if he was known to be a wee bit eccentric, then he got a tip that some newspaper reporter was sitting in the V.I.P. lounge smoking that marijuana stuff. And him waiting to interview a princess from some place out in the Middle East that was fairly swimming in oil, and that, of course, the government was sucking up to as hard as they could. So off he goes at a trot but he finds dozens of reporters puffing away like a bunch of steelwork chimneys and no telling which one was burning the dope! I personally think he should have arrested the whole lot of them and for sure, in my experience, he would have got more than a few of them with fancy plants stuffed in their pouches! That's bye the bye though, but instead he had himself a wee thought and gets a hold of one of those poor dogs that is trained to sniff the dope out. Takes it himself though, as the handler is an awful uncouth man and not to be let loose among princesses and diplomats who were also there like a flock of seagulls round a fishing boat!

'No doubt one of these uncouth Cockney fellas.' interjected Hector. 'There was one up in Dunoon last year staying at old Morag's boarding house. The uncivilized fella even put sugar on his porridge!'

'I'm surprised old Morag took a foreigner in.' Donald stated. 'I'm even more surprised that he managed to eat her porridge at all for I have it on good faith that she probably makes it out of high grade Portland cement! Still, to get on with the story.'

Donald took a few more puffs at his pipe and watched the dark smoke drift off towards the American jetty then continued. 'Just as he gets back to the exit door the princess arrives at the entrance, with all her flunkeys and bowers and scrapers and all, so he had little chance to get used to the dog or search for the drugs. Now it seems that when they were training the wee pooch, every time it found itself a bunch of drugs, it got a handful of jelly beans as a reward. Why jelly beans I don't know, but then it was an English dog, but by coincidence the princess was also very fond of jelly beans, and she was certainly not English. The dog started sniffing around, its ears shot up, its nose near twitched itself off, then it near tore the superintendent's arm off as it made a beeline across the lounge dragging the man with it! The dog had caught the scent of the sweeties in the lassies handbag and off it went scattering reporters, flunkies, diplomats and all! Tore the handbag out of the poor lassies hand and started to root around it looking for the jelly beans, and scattering the contents around for all and sundry to see!'

Donald gave a long sympathetic sigh. 'As you know Hector, no woman likes to have the contents of her handbag examined, and princesses are no exception! And here is every item being exposed and scattered and half the country's gutter press noting every little item!'

Hector almost shuddered at the thought. 'No doubt making out the worst of any item, no matter how innocent it was! Just like them, and you wonder why I don't read newspapers!'

'Not just newspapers, Hector, for it was being shown on television as well, and though they edited out a couple of bits, it was obvious that our friend Smythe Smith was the guilty party as he was lying at her feet tangled up in the dog's leash! To cut a long story short, they let the dog continue to work there as it was not the poor dumb animal's fault, but he was kicked up here well out of the way of visiting princesses!

'Hell hath no fury like a woman made look daft.' misquoted Hector solemnly. Then he grinned. 'Mind you, they should have kept him down there and sent the dog up here!'

The man being discussed was sniffing round his dismal office in Greenock when he turned round accusingly on Jimmy Thomson who was busy pounding out his report on the battered office typewriter. 'What the hell is that smell?' Smythe Smith demanded to know.

Jimmy looked up and yawned pointedly then eventually replied. 'Fish probably.' He pointed to the newspaper wrapped bundle lying by the door.

'Then it's gone off!' growled the customs super.

'Hardly likely.' contradicted Jimmy. 'Three hours ago it was swimming about in the waters of Loch Fiddin.'

'You are supposed to be watching Fiddin House!' exclaimed the superintendent. 'Not piddling around fishing in the loch!'

Jimmy held up his hands in a conciliatory gesture. 'Now hold on, super, it wasn't me that caught the fish. I got a present of a couple from the chief engineer of the Farnhead.'

'Farnhead? What the hell is the Farnhead?'

'It's the big ship that's laid up in the loch. I mentioned it to you last week when we started watching Fiddin House.'

Smythe Smith frowned as he remembered. 'It's not near the house, is it?'

Jimmy shook his head. 'A bit further up the loch, but not too far away. I cleared it when it was laid up six months back. That's when I met the chief and unfortunately in one way, he recognised me this morning in Fiddin.'

Jimmy briefly described that morning's encounter, leaving out his mention of drug smuggling. He was quite sure the super did not have his faith in Colin Cameron's discretion and need no more grief on his head than he had already.

'You're obviously completely blown over there then.' declared Smythe Smith.

'Probably.' Jimmy agreed hopefully. 'I suppose that rules me out when it comes to watching Fiddin House.'

He yawned pointedly again.

'Not necessarily!' countered the super, just as pointedly ignoring the others indication of fatigue. 'Nobody can see you at night! Now, who else is aboard this boat?'

'The size of it I think it deserves the title of ship.' Jimmy pointed out. 'I think there's usually five or six of them aboard at any one time, with one or two changing every month or so. Hector Donaldson would be able to tell you as he runs stores over to them every week.'

The super grimaced at the mention of Hector's name, for he didn't entirely trust any fisherman with his own boat, and then continued his questioning. 'I take they are all British?'

'I think they are.' Jimmy replied. 'The cook was Italian, but he's been naturalised for years now.'

'Italian!' gasped Smythe Smith. 'There's a bloody Italian up that loch and you never mentioned it before!'

'Look, super, they're not all Sicilian mafia, you know!' Jimmy jabbed his finger at the floor. 'The owners of the cafe downstairs are Italians and the hardest thing they serve is their ice cream!'

'Never liked having that lot downstairs.' whispered the custom's chief, looking round the room furtively. 'Probably trying to bug the place right now and reporting every word to some Mafia boss. It's bloody disgrace putting us up in this hotchpotch building which has no security at all!'

Jimmy gave a resigned sigh. Here he goes again, he thought. Paranoid as hell and looking for a drug dealer on every corner. 'You want me to check this Italian cook out?' he asked hopefully, figuring it would be better than spending another cold wet night on the hillside counting midges.

'No, better get some sleep, I might need you later.' the super said dashing his hopes. 'Bell should be in before long so as soon as he arrives you get home. I'm going over to Fiddin village to make a personal reconnaissance. Without attracting the attention of half the inhabitants!' he added sarcastically.

He suddenly remembered his sabotaged car. 'Damn vandals! I'll have to phone up the area office and get them to send me round another car!'

Half an hour later a quietly simmering Smythe Smith drove aboard the Fiddin ferry in a large black official looking car, hardly the quiet inconspicuous vehicle he had requested. It also was none too new and had a definite wheeze that threatened its future health. Supposedly it was the only one available but he was quite sure that he was being discriminated against by the local bunch of haggis eaters. In that respect he was probably correct, but he could hardly complain too much, for the car did run, even though the fare collector on the ferry gave it a half disgusted look as it gave a nasty cough and belched a puff of brown and smelly smoke.

Two other cars and a rather gaudy painted min-bus queued behind him waiting to board. He paid his fare and remained seated for the short crossing attempting to remain as inconspicuous as possible.

Above him the portly figure of Angus Kerr, ferry owner and captain, stalked the catwalk which supported the small wheelhouse above the vehicle deck. He suddenly stopped his impatient pacing and glared down at the gaudy mini-bus approaching the ramp.

'Gilly!' he roared down at the fare collector. 'Shut the bliddy barrier!'

Hugh Gillick, fare collector, barrier operator, deckhand, cook and general dogsbody of the Fiddin ferry, jerked his head up towards his lord and master on the bridge above. 'But there's still that mini bus to come on, skipper!'

'Shut the bliddy barrier smartish like, you damn cretin!' roared the skipper. 'I'm not having that riff-raff aboard any ship of mine!'

Gilly, well aware of his skipper's wrath and his dislikes, quickly complied and slammed the steel barrier down stranding the mini-bus on the hinged ramp between the ship and the shore. Blazoned across the sides of the gaudy vehicle were various peace symbols and slogans such as "Ban the Bomb", "Down with Cruise" and "No Subs Here", but across the front was the one which angered Angus Kerr the most, "Mothers against Polaris". He had no great dispute with the anti-nuclear movement in general, but that particular bunch had camped their ragged tents and battered caravans right outside his sister's house over on Loch Garnock, and to add insult to injury, frequently disrupted his younger brother's bus service by laying their fat stinking bodies across the road there.

Besides, most of that bunch of raggedy big mouthed women were English!

A huge tousled haired woman, apparently dressed in a couple of dozen hairy multicoloured scarves, swung down from the driver's seat of the mini-bus and confronted Gilly who stepped back smartly and kept the barrier between him and the woman who very obviously outweighed him by several boxing divisions.

'Hey you!' she bawled, waving a beefy finger in Gilly's

direction. 'What did you shut the barrier for?'

Gilly pointed upwards towards his skipper with his finger hidden behind from that direction. 'The skipper says you're not to get on, missus.'

'There's plenty of room for my bus!' the angry woman pointed out.

'Look missus, it's nothing to do with me! Captain Kerr says yer no tae get on so yer no tae get on!'

'Ms!' stated M's Bella Bolnay, crusader for women's liberation as well as numerous other causes.

Gilly, looking slightly bewildered for a moment, then attempted to apologise. 'Sorry miss, I should have known from your looks you weren't married, miss.'

Bella gave him a glare which would have turned a Greek hero to stone, but then Gilly had not really the attention span of a Greek goat herder. 'M-z-z-z!' she slowly pronounced furiously.

Gilly was maybe a bit slow and not in tune with the intricacies of the modern women's movement, but he knew anger when he saw it, and countered with some anger himself.

'Now don't you buzz at me, missus! If the skipper says yer no tae get on then no way are you getting on! Now back your old van off our ramp for we have a schedule to keep!' he added with a touch of polite and official speech which he had rehearsed many times on difficult customers.

He pointedly turned his back on her and began to cast off the mooring ropes, feeding them through their loops and pulling them onto the deck. Only the slight push of the idling engines now held the ferry against the concrete shore ramp so Gilly checked all was clear then shouted up to the bridge.

'All clear to go, skipper, apart from this gawk and her bliddy bus sitting on our ramp.'

'Fine, Gilly.' Angus Kerr shouted back. He leant over

the bridge wing and addressed himself to Bella Bolnay. 'You in your Joseph's coat of many colours, get your heap of junk off my ramp. The ferry's leaving right now!'

'Not till I'm on it!' roared back the ban the bomber. 'I'm staying right here till you lift that barrier!'

'Bliddy daft women' growled the skipper, who prided himself in running his ferry on time, though rare was the occasion when he succeeded. He turned to the third and last member of the crew who had just climbed up to the bridge to see what the disturbance was.

'Well Willie, do you think they hydraulics would lift the ramp with that van still on it?'

Willie McPhee, the ship's engineer, tapped his pipe against the side of the bridge and shook out some black ash before answering his skipper cautiously. 'I've no doubt they would, Angus, but I would not be advising it.'

'And why not, Willie, do you think the ship would fall apart with the strain?'

'The boat will be fine, Angus, it's just that I think it would be better to let them on. That lot have a lot of support from the local council which is full of left winger types just like them, and it's them we get the subsidy from.'

The skipper's face turned bright red and he puffed his cheeks up furiously. The engineer could not have hit on a sorer point. 'Bliddy council and their bliddy pittance of a subsidy! If they handed out a few bob more to me instead of handing it out to those layabouts and head cases with their banners and songs, then maybe I would be able to get a new ferry!'

Breathless with fury he stopped briefly and allowed the engineer to get a few words in. 'There is little chance of an increase if you are so choosy about your customers.'

Angus Kerr glared at him furiously. 'Och away and look after your wee engines and leave the politics to me!'

The skipper waved his hand in dismissal which on some days would have got him a hard rap on his knuckles with a big spanner just to remind him that his best friend and ship's engineer was not to be trifled with, but today, seeing the mood his skipper was in, McPhee shook his head and turned to leave. 'You are a stubborn old fool, Angus Kerr,' he muttered as he relit his pipe. 'Go ahead if you will, but no good will come of it.' He left the tiny wheelhouse and climbed down the ladder and stood outside the engine room door where he could see the hydraulics unit and switch it off if he thought it necessary.

Unhearing and uncaring the skipper turned back to the ramp again. 'Gilly! Stand clear! I'm lifting the ramp!'

He hauled on a small hydraulic lever and below the ramp began to fold itself up towards the ferry, protesting at the extra weight on it. The mini-bus front end reared up, metal grinding and tearing and Bella leapt inside with a look of horror as screams from inside echoed her own fear. The ramp continued to rise as her fear turned to fury and she whined the bus engine into life and attempted to reverse away from impending disaster. The smell of burnt rubber drifted upwards from the barely gripping front wheels but the vehicle eventually lurched backwards crashing down in a cascade of spray and rubber smoke. Up the slip way it shot erratically before abruptly stopping as it smashed into a very solid mooring bollard. The tangled figure of Bella Bolnay disappeared in a flurry of skirts as the already strained back of the driver's seat gave way with a screech and she shot backwards into a mass of her screaming followers in the back of the mini-van.

Surveying the chaos, Angus Kerr grinned broadly, well pleased with the results of his minor effort. He turned away and swung the telegraph to full ahead. The engineer was now on the main deck and looked towards the engine room door as the telegraph rang below. He reluctantly went in and slammed the door shut and a few moments later the ferry fairly leapt away into the river as its skipper endeavoured to keep up his variable time keeping record.

Chapter 4

'Very clever lads, but do you really think it will fly?'

Colin Cameron made another circuit round the small converted lifeboat which sat awkwardly on the Farnhead's deck, all the time shaking his head in mock disbelief.

'If we wanted it to fly, Chief,' said one twin. 'Then fly it would!' completed the other twin emphatically.

'But we only want it to float.' said the first twin. 'Then sink.' concluded the other in apparent contradiction.

'It's not the floating and sinking that worries me.' sighed Colin. 'It's the coming back up again!'

'Well even if it doesn't come back up again that does not stop us coming back up.' stated Michael David. 'It's not as if we'll be inside of it, only sitting on top of it.'

'And,' continued David Michael. 'It will work! You've checked every rivet and bolt yourself, Chief. We have a lot of confidence in you, and if you can't find anything wrong then there cannot be anything wrong.'

'Murphy's Law.' muttered Colin.

'Murphy's Law?' questioned the twins simultaneously.

'Murphy's Law' repeated Colin. "Anything that can go wrong, will go wrong". Named after an American aerospace engineer who worked on safety critical systems years ago. He never liked the interpretation of it himself.'

The twins looked briefly at each other, shrugged, then burst into song. 'Que sera, sera. Whatever will be, will be!'

'Okay, okay, you couple of Welsh canaries. We'll get the submarine in the water today. Go get Angelo to give us a hand.'

Triumphantly the twins danced around the deck for a few moments then split up, one to ask the cook's assistance and another to fetch a bottle of homebrew beer for a launching ceremony. The cook arrived a few minutes later and then the twins proceeded to rig the boat for lifting by the ship's stores crane. Angelo looked on warily, threw up his hands in horror at this launch of what he considered to be a totally foolhardy venture, then turned and appealed to Colin.

'Chief Cameron, you no give in to these crazy Wales boys! They get drowned and we in trouble and they finished on this ship.'

'Maybe that's why I'm letting them do it, Angelo.' Colin said mischievously. 'When we get rid of those pair of photocopies we might get a couple of normal people out here.'

'I think captain no approve of this if he sober.' Angelo pointed out.

'Hardly matters, does it? I tried to get a sensible opinion out of him this morning but he thinks it's only another lifeboat drill, even though our lifeboats are twice the size of this fiddly little thing!'

'You too soft with twins, Chief. Mr O'Hagan come back he put stop to Wales crazies! He no like them much but he no like trouble either!'

'That Angelo, is the very reason for haste. Patrick would stop them dead and they know it!' Colin shook his head sadly. 'I'm afraid the man's sense of humour does not stretch to other people enjoying themselves.'

The little cook nodded his head in agreement. He too had been a victim of O'Hagan's cruel jokes. 'Maybe he boss engineer when you leave Chief Cameron, but he try putting spaghetti in my knitting basket again and I give him a big crack on the head with frying pan!'

He gestured to where the twins were completing the task

of fitting the lifting gear on the boat. 'Maybe I give them a big crack on the head and knock some sense into them! Only crazy people go look for treasure with submarine in this loch!'

Colin laughed at the look of apprehension on the cook's face. 'Don't tell me you've been listening to the local tales of a monster in this loch! After "Nessie" was sighted a few years back half the lochs in Scotland have been trying to lay claim to a monster of their own. Good for the tourist trade, I have to admit, but hardly based on any real facts!'

The cook pointed up the deep black waters of the loch. 'Not good this place! Serve them right if they gobbled up though, even my good cooking not put enough meat on skinny Wales leeks to make one good bite!' He waved a cautionary finger at Colin. 'You no laugh when you get monster on your fishing hook!'

Colin shook his head and smiled, though out of deference to the little cook didn't laugh outright. 'Well Angelo, if I do, you had better get your biggest frying pan out and a few gallons of cooking oil because I'm going to reel the damn thing in and bring it right back for lunch!'

The little cook sighed in resignation. Nobody ever took him seriously, but then, he considered everyone at sea to be a little crazy, everyone but him, that is.

His thoughts were interrupted by a shout from one of the twins. 'All ready to lift now!'

The chief turned to Angelo. 'Give them a hand with the steadying ropes and I'll drive the crane.' He began to climb the steel ladder up to the stores crane cab.

'I pray for them, Chief Cameron!' Angelo shouted after him. 'Like I pray for all lunatics!'

Ten minutes later the self made submarine was safely sitting at the foot of the ship's gangway and the twins were checking for leaks and finding none. It was well made, and carefully, but it was doubtful if a stranger craft had ever graced the waters of the Clyde estuary, and certainly not the waters of Loch Fiddin.

It was an old small ship's lifeboat, salvaged from the local boatyard scrapheap and towed round to the ship by the twins a few months before, the short voyage only accomplished by dint of continuous bailing as the steel hull had taken some sort of battering and leaked like a kitchen sieve. The boat had been hoisted aboard the Farnhead and had remained there ever since, much against the wishes of the twins' arch enemy Patrick O'Hagan. Shortly afterwards the twins had gone home on leave, returning a few weeks later with a vanload of apparently useless scrap which they laboriously transported piece by piece on board using the ships little utility launch. Then the transformation had begun.

They spent a week carefully hammering out the dents and re-riveting the sprung seams before filling boat with water to check for leaks, finding a couple which were riveted further, caulking seams with foul mixture of modern glue and traditional tar and hemp, then filling up again till they confirmed it was it was watertight. They fitted aluminium ballast tanks that had, and properly, seen use as beer barrels. Two huge propulsion batteries had been salvaged from the remains of an old Cardiff Cooperative milk float whose driver had been sampling other stuff than his liquid products. The batteries had survived a forty foot drop from a bypass flyover, the driver had not.

The propellers electric motors had at one time run fairground dodgem cars and the powerful underwater lights had last shone in a short lived sea aquarium whose manager was now enjoying the sun on a Brazilian beach, courtesy of some very disenchanted investors. From near and far the twins had collected their bits and pieces and all amazingly began to fit together.

Colin had lent a hand on several occasions but he had to admit that design and construction was almost pure Welsh. Like a mechanic's version of a fire breathing dragon though in this case it breathed light.

Between raids on local boat and scrap yards much welding, hammering and riveting took place as batteries and motor had been fitted into sealed compartments, air tanks and transfer valves fitted and tested, controls added, removed for adaptation, and refitted again. Then the deck had been closed in with thin steel plate, a couple of frame seats added, and a control panel fitted in front of it. Colin had checked and tested everything along the way and had to admit there was very little he could fault, though he shuddered at the unconventional look of the craft. No doubt even the toughest German U Boat commander would have done the same, yet there it was, floating at the side of the Farnhead, being checked over again by the twins.

Both were accomplished scuba divers and though Colin still had doubts about the safety of the entire project, never mind the sanity, he was secretly proud of his contribution, small though it might be. And confident in the ability of the twins to get back safely as well even if the crazy sub did sink!

It had all started one night in the local pub when a visiting historian had told the twins about the lost treasure of Prince Charles Edward Stuart. Now Bonny Prince Charlie had never been near Loch Garnock where the treasure was reputed to be, nor had laid eyes on the treasure bearing his name, and it was doubtful if he had ever even heard of that loch. But add that romantic name of his to the lure of even supposed gold and a legend was quickly born.

Supposedly collected in Ireland by Jacobite sympathisers and shipped to Scotland where the carrying craft had been sunk by an English frigate; the location was as imprecise as the rest of the story but, generally accepted to be within Garnock waters. To there, for two hundred plus years, legend lovers and treasure seekers had flocked, all returning home no richer and seldom any wiser. Only a few local hoteliers and boat hirers had made money out of the legends, and every year spent a great deal of time filling the reporters of various newspapers with a great deal of whisky and imaginative rumour in a bid to keep the dubious legend alive and kicking.

The twins had their own theory. The previous treasure hunters had been looking in the wrong loch.

'Think it out logically.' one of them told him one night. 'Charlie boy was away to the east in the direction of Stirling, so, if you wanted to fill his sporran with gold, why land it in a loch to the west of here? That would mean an extra hundred miles or so of wilderness without roads to get to where he was. If they landed it on the east shore of Loch Fiddin they would have avoided that.'

Colin had to admit their logic was fine; it was difficult enough to get to Stirling by road from Loch Garnock these days, in 1745, near impossible if laden with treasure. He tried to point out that the English frigate could have chased them up Loch Garnock before ripping the treasure ship apart but got knocked back by more logic.

'The Yanks apparently spent months surveying the bottom of Garnock with the best of equipment before bringing their nukes here. If there had been a wrecked ship there, they would have found it!'

The matter rested at that. They intended to use their home made submarine to search the deep dark waters of Fiddin to test their theory, and as theories go, one was as good as the other.

He had to agree that building the sub had helped pass the time, which hung heavily on everyone's hands on the laid up vessel. Now the end result lay waiting. He descended the gangway for the naming ceremony but refused to do the honours.

'You pair built it.' he told the twins. 'So too you should go the honour of naming it.'

They grinned back at him. 'That's fine then, Chief, we rather wanted to anyhow.' They grasped the bottle of homebrew between them and precariously hung over the bow of the sub. 'We name this ship Thetis.' they said in chorus, and smashed the bottle against the sharp vee of the reinforced bow.

'Thetis?' queried Colin. 'Wasn't that the name of the submarine that sank in Liverpool Bay during the Second World War?'

'Yes Chief.' chorused the twins. 'Our grandfather worked on it just before it sank. We're naming the sub in his honour.'

'Jesus wept!' exclaimed the astounded Chief Engineer. 'Angelo is right; the pair of you are crazy!'

Smythe Smith was at that moment checking out the village of Fiddin and missed the launching of the Thetis, just as he missed the near launching of the Mothers against Polaris van at the ferry slip, such was his angry focus. Mainly he was now looking for the Italian cook from the Farnhead or anyone else who looked vaguely like a smuggler of drugs, or even more vaguely like he looked out of place in the quiet village. At that time of the day though the only people in Fiddin were the people of Fiddin itself, and they didn't look vague or smuggled. The only suspicious character in the place was Smythe Smith himself.

He had parked his car by the pub then trekked through the village towards the rough track which led steeply up the hillside past the manse and the church. He puffed a bit as he skirted the old graveyard, its silent stones bearing no names like his own, and no doubt the souls of the departed shuddered as one of the "Auld Enemy" passed the resting place of their patriotic bodies, but the customs man was anything but a spiritual person and gave it not a thought. The vantage point used by the other customs men lay just beyond and gave an unobstructed view across the loch to the big house and the angular hulk of the Farnhead. The heather was slightly damp from the earlier dew and he removed part of his morning paper from his pocket, spread it on a raised hummock and proceed to make himself comfortable. Binoculars in hand and lying full length looking over the hummock he swept the loch, first focussing on the whitewashed mass of Fiddin House, totally unaware of the big busted beauty looking up at him from the open page three below his elbows.

After a few minutes scanning he saw nothing moving and was about to shift his gaze to the big bulk carrier when a voice from behind nearly frightened him out of his breakfast.

'Filthy pervert!' screeched none other than the lady of the manse, coming back from her morning stroll and spotting the naked woman stretched below the customs man.

Shocked, Smythe Smith rolled over, placing his elbow firmly into a still wet pile of sheep's droppings. 'Oh damn it! Oh bloody shit!' he cried in disgust as a swarm of bluebottles steamed up from the pile.

'Blasphemer!' screamed the woman, the voice rising to fever pitch. 'Filthy peeping Tom!

The minister wife stood over him like an avenging angel, if ever angels had such a sour face, waving a wicked looking knurled walking stick.

'I can assure you madam,' cried Smythe Smith, attempting to struggle to his feet, face flushed with embarrassment. 'I am no peeping Tom!'

'Liar! Pervert! Blasphemer.' she screamed, taking a stride towards him, stick flicking out and catching the obvious evidence of his sins in the air, the wind catching the page three girl and whirling it down the slope.

He stumbled backwards, ever mindful of that knotty cudgel and the avenging look on this harridan's face, tripped over a clump of bracken, and landed butt down and very firmly on a wet pile left there by an overgenerous highland cow. An even bigger swarm of angry disturbed bluebottles and flies buzzed up from his rear adding to those already circling him and near driving him demented.

'Hell's bells!' he screamed in panic. 'More shit!'

The minister's wife stepped back with a look of horror on her face then pocked out with her stick nearly taking him right on the chin. 'In the filth you should be!' she screamed. 'The filth on your body matches the filth of your mind and the filth of your mouth!'

Smythe Smith sat there gulping in fear of that waving stick trying to think of a suitable repost and failing before she again poked it towards him,

'I should thrash you for your filth,' she snarled at him. 'But I know the Lord himself will hand out far worse punishment to you on judgement day!'

She withdrew the stick slightly and the customs man gave a gasp of relief and stuttered out what he hoped was a defence. 'I-I -am an officer of Her Majesty's Customs and Excise!' he exclaimed in panic. 'I'm watching that ship for drug smugglers!'

'Liar! You were peeping in the windows of Fiddin House!'

Smythe Smith, the physical threat seemingly withdrawn, was now getting angry. 'That thief is under suspicion as well!'

The air fairly whistled through Mrs MacIver's teeth as

she sharply sucked in her breath, and then her words spat out in a vicious verbal assault 'You! A miserable perverted creature like you, would dare to accuse Sir John of dealing in the devil's drugs! And him the very man that paid for most of the new roof on the Lord's place of worship!'

The walking stick swung again and then jabbed within a few inches of Smythe Smith setting of further panic. 'I'm a customs man!' he shouted fearfully, fumbling out and flourishing his identity card. The card was immediately flicked from his hand by a stroke that would have won an Olympic medal and went spinning down the hillside.

'Then take your filthy customs and your filthy English pornography and get out of this glen before the Lord strikes you down for your evil ways!'

Smythe Smith knew he was defenceless against this woman and, not so much terrified by God as that wild flashing cudgel in front of him, grabbed the remnants of his paper and stumbled sticky and stinky legged away towards the village.

'I will set my dogs on you if you ever show your face in Glen Fiddin again! Mrs MacIver screamed after him. 'They will soon pick up the scent of a filthy sinner like you!'

Commander Barnaby Lewis Clarke filed letter two hundred and twenty-five from the Mothers against Polaris and slammed shut the steel grey cabinet with noisy vindictiveness. One damn letter every day since that mob of harridans had turned up and camped by the jetty gates. One every day, to answer politely and sincerely, as was official policy of the United States Navy. Every day, half his day wasted writing to crazies!

He kicked out in disgust at his empty waste paper basket. It should be full and the filing cabinet empty! Then maybe he would be able to get down to his proper job of catching spies!

He dialled the lookout on the ships gangway. 'Seaman Padowski back aboard yet?'

'Yes Sir! Came back about fifteen minutes ago.'

'Locate him and send him up to see me.'

'Will do, Commander. By the way sir, did you happen to have breakfast this morning?'

'I did. Why?' asked the puzzled Commander, thinking that somebody at least was concerned about his comfort. He was quickly disillusioned.

'Well sir, you know that black pudding stuff that the cook's started serving up? Some guy told me it was made with pig's blood! I ain't felt so good since then sir. You sure that's the kind of stuff we Americans should be eating?'

Clarke gritted his teeth. This was another rubbish job he was supposed to supervise but he was not in the mood. 'Jesus Christ, if you don't like the goddamn stuff, then don't eat it! Those goddamn Jocks stuff it down their gullets by the ton and it doesn't seem to do them any harm!'

'If you don't mind me saying so Commander, they eat all sorts of crap which may not be healthy. Some kind of bird they call a haggis which they cook by stuffing inside a sheep brains!'

Clarke shook his head and felt like thumping it hard against his desk but knew he had to try to keep calm. 'I don't think that is quite what haggis is, but by all means ask some Jock about it if you really want to know. In the meantime, stick to burgers and find me Padowski!'

The commander slammed the phone down and screwed up his eyes in mental pain. This was turning out to be a bitch of a day with every moan possible thrown his way. He lashed out at the poor uncomplaining waste paper basket again sending it spinning across the small cabin. It came to rest just as there was a knock at the door and Padowski entered, near fell over the basket, side stepped over it quickly and picked it up at the same time throwing a sloppy salute with his other hand. Clarke threw an equally sloppy reply then gestured to Padowski to be seated. The seaman sat down awkwardly, the waste bin in his lap.

'Put the goddamn bin down.' sighed Clarke. 'Unless you intend to throw up in it or something.'

At that moment, and every other time he had to meet the commander, Padowski did feel like throwing up. Purely nervous reaction to impending doom in the shape of stopped shore passes, but a real enough feeling. He put the bin down though well clear of his own feet.

Lewis Clarke glowered at him, taking the morning's spite out on someone he knew dare not fight back. 'Okay, so you finally made it back. Now what's been happening with those commies in the boat?'

Padowski shifted uncomfortably in the chair, well aware that he had not a lot to report. 'The old guy was early this morning,' he said. 'But I think that was just to give him time to refuel.'

'Well he had to sometime! He's not got a nuke pushing that heap of junk! Did you manage to follow him?'

'Well, almost everywhere.' replied the uneasy Padowski.

'Where's everywhere?'

'After he refuelled the boat at the quay he headed up into town, bought some pipe tobacco at a newsagents shop then cut across the square into the older part of the town.'

Padowski hesitated knowing the commander was not going to like this and glanced around but seen no way to escape. The commander fixed cobra like eyes on the squirming prey before him. 'Get on with it!'

Padowski gritted his teeth. 'I'm sorry sir, but that's where I lost him.' he blurted out. 'You have to understand sir; it's like a rabbit warren up there. He turned into one of those real narrow alleyways and just vanished!'

The furious commander thumped his desk and the unfortunate waste paper basket was once more kicked across the room. 'Damn you, Padowski! That's three times you've lost him!'

'But I picked him up again when he left, sir!' the seaman added hurriedly 'The other old guy was with him and they both went back to the boat!'

'You goddamn piece of hogs ass! I know they went back to the boat. I know the boat came over here! I know it's sitting out there now! What I want to know is where they hang out in Greenock!'

Clarke again thumped the desk and lashed out at the waste basket and nearly fell of his chair when his foot failed to find any resistance as the basket had apparently crept far enough away to avoid any more abuse.

'If you can't find a simple thing like that,' the commander continued. 'Then there is no point in you being across there. There's no point in me giving out passes so there's no more nights going to be spent with your floozie!'

'Gimme one more chance, Commander' pleaded the seaman. 'I'll find out for sure tomorrow! Just one more chance?'

He played his ace card at that point, hoping it might be enough to get him off the hook. 'I found out the old guy's name, and where he comes from!'

He hurriedly related his conversation with the bystander down at the quay and watched Clarke's face take on a sneaky look.

'Comes from Fiddin, you reckon?' mused the commander. 'Okay, I'll check that out myself. You get one more chance but if you foul that up ---.'

He left the threat unsaid but Padowski knew exactly what it was and nodded frantically in compliance.

'Go see Maitland and get another pass for tonight then.' Clarke spat out. 'And don't even bother coming back if you screw up!'

He dismissed the seaman who hurried out fairly leaping over the much abused basket then sat back to think on the received information. Time to pay a visit to the village of Fiddin, but it would have to be later. He cursed quietly to himself. Just time to get some grub and then back to the dreary grind of the afternoons work as welfare officer.

'Shit!' he moaned in despair. 'Grown men crying on my shoulder!'

Smythe Smith was shortly afterwards sitting at a very similar steel desk cursing in the same manner, though on a totally separate subject than his American counterpart across the river.

'Damn these Scottish madmen, and damn their crazy women as well!' he muttered quietly.

He blushed furiously at his humiliation. Though he had changed both his jacket and trousers at his flat before he returned to his office, he was sure he could still detect the sickening odour of both sheep and cow manure lingering about his person. No doubt, while he was still wearing the soiled garments, the ferryman who had taken his return ticket had also detected the smell. The expression on the man's face when he opened the car window had made that very clear. The whole damn area would probably know by now as he had been observed by several nose wrinkling people as he made his way back to the car and headed rapidly for the ferry and the comparative safety and anonymity of the other side of the river.

To make things worse he knew he would have to return

to find his identity card as losing one of them was no small matter in the Customs service. Smythe Smith shuddered at the thought of stepping back into that village, even quietly under the cover of darkness as he intended, then cursed quietly again.

Terry "Tinkle" Bell, junior Custom's officer, looked up from the papers on his desk for the first time since he attempted to give his superior officer a civil greeting some twenty minutes before. That had been answered by little less than a snarl so he had discreetly held his peace up till now. Still, he had a few things to ask his boss so it might be as well now as later.

'You said something, super?' he enquired tentatively.

'Harrumph. No. Just thinking aloud.'

'You want me to go and watch the Big House tonight?'

'No!' replied Smythe Smith realising that he would be over in that area. 'But I want you to go to Fiddin this afternoon. Make a few enquiries. You know the place well?'

'I do that, super. My mother came from Fiddin and I spent most of my summers over there when I was a boy.'

'Then get the ferry across, ask around, but don't let anyone know what you are up to.'

The superintendent gave Bell detailed instructions on how Bell should conduct his enquires, hoping to steer the other man away from any revelations of that morning's personal fiasco.

'Be discreet, but find out everything you can about that ship laid up in the loch, and her crew. But do not approach any of them if they are ashore, I don't want them to know you are sniffing around!'

'Don't worry about that, super, I know the very person to ask about them.' said Tinkle with a smile. 'Talking about sniffing though, what's the funny smell that's hanging around the office today?'

Smythe Smith blushed furiously. 'Nothing but your imagination! Now get out of here and catch that bloody ferry!'

Chapter 5

It was much later in the day, when the Dhu Mohr left her anchorage and headed back to Greenock, before Lewis Clarke decided it was safe to go ashore unobserved. It was evening and though hardly dark, the shadows from the steep hills to the east gave he and his assistant a cloak of anonymity as they crossed to the base landing pier in the liberty boat. Gil Maitland Junior, even though he was the crew representative of the two man welfare committee, seldom felt any compulsion to accompany the other member of the committee on his nocturnal ventures but had noted the generous provision of shore passes to the love stricken Padowski and, being a blue blooded Southern boy who fancied himself with the local ladies, he had decided he wanted a bit of the action himself. If that meant the occasional sortie in the wilds of the Highlands with his half cracked commander, then so be it. It was not too much of a price to pay, or so he thought.

'Pick up the keys for a Jeep.' ordered the commander as they climbed up onto the jetty. 'We might be hitting some rough territory tonight!'

He gave a derogatory glance at the Country and Western type garb of the seaman. 'Though by the look of you it should be a horse you're picking up!'

Maitland, totally unperturbed by his commanders observation just shrugged. 'Well sir, you said to dress casual, and this is about as casual as I have.'

He hurried off to collect the Jeep keys from the gatehouse before the conventionally dressed commander could reply. A couple of minutes later he rejoined him and swung casually into the seat of one of several veteran four wheel drive Navy Grey coloured vehicles.

'Where to, Commander' he enquired.

'Head for Fiddin. We're gonna half a good look round the place then have a couple of drinks in the local bar. See what information I can pick up there.'

'Wouldn't mind a couple of beers.' said Maitland hopefully.

'That's real tough shit then sailor!' stated the commander callously. 'You're driving so you ain't drinking! Besides, you have to watch the Jeep. Don't want some commie son of a bitch sneaking up on us and sabotaging it!'

'Goddamn pig assed officers!' Maitland swore under his breath, accelerating the Jeep away viciously sending the commander cracking against the unforgiving seat back. He swung out of the compound and secretly hoped the pub would be shut before they got there, and swung across the road in a sharp turn that sent a shrapnel burst of loose gravel rattling against the side of some gaudily painted caravans and tents of the dreaded Mothers against Polaris.

Some thirty minutes later, his brief reconnaissance of the almost darkened village completed and Maitland Jnr. left outside with the Jeep, Lewis Clarke was enjoying the relaxed atmosphere of the local inn and chatting with its host and only barman. Though not over-enamoured of American servicemen who occasionally visited his establishment, the owner did not mind at all who he spoke to, as long as they were providing him with the large whisky now held in his hand.

'Cheers sir.' said the publican, raising his glass to the commander. 'You will be off one of those submarine things then?'

Lewis Clarke raised his glass in a return salute. 'No, Bayou Leaf.'

'Certainly. Carry on.' the puzzled publican said. Strange people these Yanks, he thought, but courteous in their own way. He raised his glass again. 'By your leave too, sir.'

'That's my ship.' said an equally confused Lewis Clarke.

'And I was thinking that all you sub mariners called them boats.' the publican said. 'Or maybe it's just the British that do that.' He caught the even more confused look on the commander's face and decided to close that subject. 'Well, it is of no importance. There are a lot of strange things happen in this world.'

Lewis Clarke was not that confused that he didn't see the perfect opening, and jumped right in. 'Anything strange happening around here?'

The publican took another sip of his whisky and seemed to stare in contemplation at the dark wood beams of the ceiling. 'Well now, there was my grandmother's great grandfather who went for a walk up the loch side one day. And a fine walk it is too, especially in the springtime when the snow is still on the hills and the burns are in full spate tumbling down into the loch from the corries and cliff tops. Of course it is fine in September as well when the heather is all purple and brown and---'

'So what happened to the guy?' interrupted an impatient Lewis Clarke.

'You mean my grandmother's great grandfather? Well he never came back, you see.' the publican took another sip of his whisky and continued. 'Some weeks later some lad, I think it was one of the McFarlanes from round at Loch Garnock, found his head, chopped off neat like, sitting there on a stone at the side of the loch.'

Lewis Clarke gulped a big shot of his whisky down and stared at the relaxed publican who seemed totally unmoved by the horror he was describing. 'This was one of your ancestors? Did they ever find the rest of him?'

The publican shrugged. 'Never at all, and that is why there are some that say that the Fiddin monster ate him, and then spat his head out for it did not want all that hair mixed with its food!' The publican smiled as if he didn't believe all that superstitious nonsense. 'Personally I think it was one of those wild MacGregors that live up at the top of the glen that cut his head off. They had a grudge against him for throwing a couple of them out of the pub one night when they started to give him abuse about the name of the place.'

Lewis Clarke had seen the sign over the door when he entered and had wondered a bit about it himself. It stated boldly "The Londoners Arms" and he didn't imagine that Londoners were all that popular around here.

'It's a kind of strange name.' he said cautiously, thinking on heads being cut off. 'Did your ancestor come from London then?'

The publican threw down the last of his whisky and waved his hands in horror and the commander realised he might just have insulted him badly. He hurriedly asked the man to have another drink and when the publican poured a large one and Lewis Clarke paid for it and his own; the man eventually appeared to calm down a little.

'No English in my family, sir! Not a drop of English blood in my veins despite the pub's name. The whole family from way back were born and bred in Fiddin!'

Lewis Clarke cautiously asked why the pub had the name though and the publican grinned and answered with a mellow look that indicated that the story had been often told before.

'Well sir, it appears that my grandmother's great, great, grandfather, or thereabouts, set out with a few others from the village to follow Prince Charles Edward Stuart when he invaded England back in '45, but when the rest turned back at Derby, he just carried onto London. Not out of any great patriotism though, as really he did not support the Stuart cause much, but by all accounts he was a shrewd man who realised that England seemed to have more money in it than Scotland had at the time and, of course, London would have more again. And after all, the Young Pretender was not all that good at paying his common foot soldiers! Besides, and quite rightly to considering that a lot of people from round here got put to the sword at Culloden, it seemed a bit less risky than hanging around with a loser!'

Lewis Clarke, a patriotic man himself, couldn't really understand this, but certainly didn't want to risk falling out with this publican who had on display behind the bar, a lot of large pieces of sharp cutlery and shields with spiky edges, some of which looked like they had seen a bit of wear and tear.

'Did he do well?' he asked in a neutral as possible tone.

'He got himself into the liquor trade down there, that is, he began to sell those poor Londoners whisky that he had distilled himself using an old family recipe. Made a fair bit of cash with it as well as giving those Sassenachs a goodly few hangovers, and then came back here and built himself an inn.'

Lewis Clarke gave a wry smile. 'Named it after the mugs who supplied the money?'

'That's partly right, sir, but also there were a lot of English soldiers crawling around the hills by then looking for sympathisers of the Prince and he thought it best to keep in with them.'

'So this place has been in the family ever since?'

'Not quite this place. The original inn burnt down some hundred years ago and my great grandfather rebuilt it on the same site. That was about the last excitement the village had.'

'And nothing strange has been happening recently?'

'Nothing much at all. Mind you, the minister was telling me earlier that earlier today some foreigner was up on the hillside with a pair of binoculars and was spying on the loch with them!'

Lewis Clarke nearly choked on his drink. After all the rambling around finally he had something for his trouble. 'Foreigner? Spying on the loch?'

'That would be right, sir. On the hillside above the old graveyard. Mrs MacIver, that is the minister's wife, she herself saw the man and his binoculars. Soon sent him packing though!'

The publican could see the American's keen interest and also the relative emptiness of both of their glasses, so he gestured towards the gantry. 'Would you be wanting another dram, sir?'

'Sure, yes! A bit of ice in mine. And have one yourself.'

The publican busied himself with the drinks while Lewis Clarke tried to visualise the layout of the village and the surrounding hills. He was almost certain that the submarine base would be visible from the hilltop.

'Cheers.' the publican said as he returned with the refilled glasses. 'That will be two pounds fifty, sir.'

The commander returned the salute and paid the required amount without even thinking about how much he was being overcharged.

'Which loch was he watching, Fiddin or Garnock?' he asked.

'Och man, would I be asking the minister a question like that?' huffed the publican. 'If Mr MacIver said "the loch" it would almost certainly be our loch he was speaking off. Mind you, Loch Garnock would be visible from the top of the hill but if you were wanting a good view of that you would be better off on the road at the top of Glen Garnock.'

'How much of Loch Garnock could you see from the top

of the hill though.' persisted Lewis Clarke.

'More or less from end to end, but it was never much of a view, and, no offence to you, sir, since your lot filled it up with all sorts of lumps of iron, it has not improved any! Now the view of Loch Fiddin from there is a different matter. Hardly a finer one in Scotland. On a clear summer's day---.'

The commander interrupted, seeing the faraway look in the publican's eyes and not wanting a long rambling description of Highland scenery.

'The man with the binoculars! Did this Mrs MacIver say anything about him?'

'Well maybe she did, then maybe she did not. I can only say what the minister himself told me.' He paused for a moment and pointedly drained his glass and gave Lewis Clarke a hopeful look.

'Not for me.' the commander said glancing down at his barely touched whisky with its solitary half melted ice cube. 'But have another yourself.'

'I will that, sir, thank you. Thirsty work all this talking.' He hurried off to refill his glass.

Lewis Clarke could hardly contain his excitement. A foreigner with binoculars! It hardly mattered what loch they thought he had been watching. The goddamn Ruskies could maybe fool these locals but not this smart American kid! The place could be swarming with commie spies and these Highland Hillbillies would think they were only bird watching. He paid the publican for the drink and hastily continued his questioning. 'So what about this guy on the hill?'

'Well sir, it seems he tried to claim he was something official but Mrs MacIver was having nothing to do with that! Tried to show her some sort of identity card but she just knocked it out of his hand and sent it flying down the hill. You understand, sir, she is not the kind of woman you would be wanting to argue with, a woman to put the fear of God in any man!'

He took a sip at his drink, realising that maybe he couldn't push his luck much further, then he continued. 'Now the minister himself is a different kettle of fish, a real gentleman even though he is not from Fiddin. Only been here some twenty-five years. I remember fine the day he arrived on Big Ian's fishing boat. It was one of those drab days that we get every now and again and the loch--.'

Lewis Clarke interrupted again. 'What happened to the foreigner?'

'Oh him? Well most of the village saw him passing through, a bit dirty and dishevelled, and muttering away to himself in some heathen tongue. He had parked his car just along the road there, a big black official looking thing. Was away in a flash and I heard he caught the next ferry back to Greenock.'

'What happened to the identity card?' the commander asked.

'Well the minister told me that he was in such a panic to escape the wrath of Mrs MacIver that he never even bothered to pick it up. It's probably still lying up there in the heather littering the place up.'

Lewis Clarke almost whooped in triumph. At last! A chance to get some documentary proof of a commie spy ring!

Ten minutes later he was back in the jeep feeling well boosted up. Having bought the publican another appreciatory consumed double whisky he had managed to pin down a reasonably accurate position for the earlier confrontation, in between enthusiastic descriptions of the local scenery in winter and summer, in rain and in snow, and even the bright tropical weather which the publican insisted was the norm for the entire year. This despite the dreariness of Greenock, and the freezing rain which he knew as normal, just round the corner in Loch Garnock.

As Lewis Clarke exited the inn, two locals, not suntanned at all, entered the bar and enquired after the hastily departing American.

'It is only these daft underwater people from the base in Loch Garnock.' the publican told them. 'Then the Loch Garnock lot always were a bit fishy.'

'Och!' exclaimed one of the locals in disgust. 'I can almost smell the fish! Between the Americans tonight and the Englishman earlier on, the place is being fairly overrun by bliddy foreigners!'

Gil Maitland Jnr. had sat patiently in the jeep trying to look inconspicuous, sipping a can of Coca Cola and listening to the strident tones of Johnny Cash on his portable cassette player. He was aware of a few strange looks but ignored them. If the locals did not like the Man in Black, that was their problem. It never even entered his mind that the looks were little to do with the music and more to do with an apparent cowboy sitting outside the village pub in an obvious American Navy Jeep.

'Shut that goddamn thing off!' ordered Lewis Clarke as he climbed into the jeep. 'You'll wake half the village with that racket.'

Maitland frowned slightly at that but the goddamn thing was duly shut off.

'We've got the commies this time!' Lewis Clarke crowed, launching into a short version of the events relayed by the publican. 'It's probably the son of a bitch's diplomatic passport he was waving around and now it's lying up there on the hill. They wave the damn things around every time one of them gets caught with their fingers the least bit sticky, so it would be whipped out pronto when that dame gave him some hassle. Guess he panicked and I don't blame him. That minister's wife sounds like a real mean dragon!'

He started to rumble about beneath the seats and soon produced two large heavy flashlights.

'Let's go find the damn commie's documents. That will give the CIA's dickheads something to think about!'

The seaman suspected that maybe his superior had just a little too much of Scotland's premier product in him but dare not say so, but tried using logic instead. 'You mean like now, sir? In the dark, sir? There's all sorts of rocks and cliffs up there sir and I really think maybe we should come back when it's daylight, sir?'

'And have some damn billygoat chew the thing up for its breakfast? No way! We go now!'

'They don't have goats up this way, Commander. It's sheep they have around here.'

'I don't care if it's goddamn ostriches!' Lewis Clarke exclaimed sternly shoving one torch into Maitland's hand. 'Now get your butt off that seat and get moving!'

It was a sixty mile drive round from Greenock to the east side of Loch Garnock but Smythe Smith would have driven six hundred rather than make the short ferry trip and even shorter drive through the village of Fiddin. He had called off the night watch of Fiddin House, 'A new line of enquiry to pursue.' he had told Sergeant Donaldson on the latter's return from the watch on the American base. 'Mustn't tire the troops out you know.'

He had of course not mentioned his earlier humiliation nor his intention to sneak back to the hillside that night to recover his identity card.

The neck of land between Lochs Garnock and Fiddin was less than a mile wide at the point Smythe Smith intended to cross, and according to the ordnance survey map he had bought, a rough track led across from a farmhouse on the Garnock road to the village of Fiddin and right past the old graveyard where his card had been lost. The moon was up and would make the trek across easy, or so he hoped. His card had a fluorescent holder so would show up easily by the light of the big heavy torch he had.

'Damn that crazy woman!' he muttered to himself as he drove down past the American base. The usual Marine guards stood casually by the gates and across the road the shanty town of the Mothers against Polaris sat, fires flickering in the darkness and the sound of guitars and protest songs still twanging away into the night.

'Bloody loonies!' he muttered in passing. 'I wouldn't be surprised if it wasn't one of them that attacked me today!'

He made a mental note to someday carry out a raid on the protest camp, feeling sure he would pick up a few miscellaneous drugs in the process. Bitterly he regretted that he would be unable to make a raid at the same time on the American base as he felt sure he could pick up an even bigger haul there! Still, just let him catch one of the beggars ashore with drugs and he would throw the book at them, so called allies or not!

A circling patrol boat swept its searchlight over the calm waters of the loch, momentarily picking out the outline of a fat black sinister hull against the Polaris mother ship. Like a whale calf suckling against its mother. Only a very lethal and very radioactive whale calf.

The custom's man shuddered slightly. He imagined the lethal cargo of missiles in the hands of some dope crazed maniac. The world at the mercy of junkies! Smythe Smith regarded half the American nation as junkies and a goodly portion of their armed forces. Hadn't that lot in Vietnam been blasted out of their minds on dope? The privates there would be generals now and the sailors, captains of nuclear submarines! He drove on quickly putting as much distance as possible between himself and his imagined horrors and was soon well down the east side of the loch.

Fifty yards short of the path to Glen Fiddin he pulled into a convenient lay-by and checked his equipment. One stout walking stick, a British army surplus compass to go with the quarter inch survey map, and a surreptitiously borrowed rubber clad torch from Sergeant Donaldson's desk drawer. Carefully he locked the car doors and switched on the torch. The beam snapped on, then off again, then back on! Then it settled down to an irregular flickering. He cursed and shook it violently but to no avail. The flickering continued. One would have thought that a stolen policeman's torch would have been reliable!

He blushed slightly at the thought of "stolen". It was borrowed, only borrowed. His own fault, he should have asked the sergeant. He resigned himself to the flickering torch and set off up the darkened path.

By daylight the path up the side of the Burrie Burn was a pleasant enough walk, cutting past Daft Doug's farmhouse just after it left the lochside road. These tumbled down group of buildings lay in a crook of the stream and had lacked repair for some thirty years or more. Daft Doug no longer held tenure of the hillside nor of the low lying land by the loch shore though, at one time, considerable land had been attached to the farm. Only a few scrappy acres surrounding the farm buildings had been retained along with a weird collection of domestic and farm animals scattered through various pens and sheds.

All the other land had been sold, some at premium prices including the area by the American landing dock, all repairs had been indefinitely postponed, and all thoughts of running the farm as a going concern forgotten to indulge Daft Doug's obsession with old clocks. Grandfather clocks, grandmother clocks, alarm clocks, cuckoo clocks, water clocks, electric, air driven, gas driven or plain clockwork, it mattered little. Let it whir, tick, hiss or drip, as long as it turned hands round a dial, Daft Doug would buy it, love it, and treasure it.

Nobody knew how many he had collected, and it was doubtful if he knew himself, but every antique dealer within a hundred miles had heard of the collection and had at one time or another beat a path to the farmhouse with hopes of making a killing. But not any longer, for as his collection grew, so did the ferocity with which Daft Doug defended it. Many a dealer had though he could convince a simple farmer to buy a heap of old junk or swap it for a real treasure and found that it was not so easy at all. The only killing that was nearly made was to themselves as they fled from the farmyard pursued by the business end of a twelve bore double barrelled shotgun!

Smythe Smith had not been informed of this trivial fact, mainly because he had not told anyone of his intentions. Still, the path lay on the opposite bank of the burn until far up the hillside then crossed just before the steep corrie running down from Ben Burr so likely it would have been safe enough, and so it proved for the uphill journey. The path though was full of pitfalls, easily avoided in good light, but in the dark almost unaided by the ever flickering torch they were often ready to snatch a pair of feet away. Smythe Smith fell into ditches, stumble over needling whin bushes and cracked his shins on treacherously jutting rocks several times before he reached the small stone bridge over the burn. Beyond the bridge the track curved over the heather clad hill to the vantage point overlooking Glen Fiddin before turning south to the village. Dark clouds flitted over the moon, as the superintendent crested the hill, bathing the slope eerily and alternately in cold light and dark shadow as the torch continued its sporadic flickering as he stumbled downhill searching for his identity card.

But he was not the only person on the hillside making

that search, for two more were now making their way towards an inevitable collision over the missing identity card.

'Up there, Commander!' exclaimed Maitland Jnr. 'Some guys signalling with a light!'

'Keep your goddamn voice down!' hissed the sweating Lewis Clarke as he struggled up the rough track behind the seaman. 'And put your flashlight out! We don't want to scare the commies off.'

The two huddled together on the now dark hillside 'Okay, Maitland,' ordered the commander. 'You move off the path and around to the left and I'll cut round to the right and we've got the son of a bitch trapped. As soon as I whistle, we jump in and grab him!'

Maitland Jnr. sounded none too happy about that. 'Commander, maybe we should just watch. He might be armed!'

'Don't turn chicken on me!' hissed Lewis Clarke. 'This is England; they don't run around with six shooters and tomahawks here.'

'Hate to correct you sir, but this is Scotland, and if this is a Ruskie, he's liable to be carrying half an arsenal around with him!'

'Stop picking faults you goddamn Southern yellow belly! Any blue bloodied American can sort out ten goddamn Ruskies, armed or not! Now get moving or see how you like cleaning out the bilges on the ship!'

Stung by his remarks and having no wish to make acquaintance with any ships bilges, Maitland Jnr. pulled himself together. 'No need to get personal, Commander, but just remember this. When they bury me I want the Confederate flag draped over my coffin!'

With that last remark the seaman slipped off into the night and apart from a few muttered curses from high up on the hill the night turned silent and dark.

Smythe Smith had reached the gentler slopes of the path and peered down towards the few lights of the village and took his bearings from that. 'Just about there.' he murmured. 'My card must be just beyond those whin bushes.'

He moved down a few more steps and the torch gave out again but the moon glinting off the loch gave him enough light to see the whins and he began to part them to search beyond. Then the light sprang on again.

The beam caught Maitland Jnr. full in the face lighting it up like a glowing skull. Smythe Smith screamed in terror at the glowing startled visage, and then the torch went out again. He sprang backwards, feet fighting through the heather towards the hill crest but a burly figure hurled itself at him and the two entwined men tumbled down the hill crushing the whin bushes and the unfortunate seaman behind them.

'Get the son of a bitch!' screamed the commander, struggling with the terrified customs man.

The sound of an American voice brought fresh terror to Smythe Smith. Yankee dope dealers! American Mafia! Ruthless killers! His terror gave him strength and he jerked his knee upwards and smashed it brutally into his attacker's groin.

The agonised commander screamed out a high pitched protest at this abuse and fell back heavily onto Maitland Jnr. and both fell back into the helpless and guiltless whin bushes. Smythe Smith struggled free and staggered up the hill, dropping torch, compass and walking stick and caring nought about direction or hazards in his frantic flight. Below the Americans lay moaning in the darkness for a few moments before managing to disentangle and begin a slow painful pursuit.

'Goddamn commie tried to blind me!' swore Maitland Jnr. as he struggled upwards ripping bits of whin from his clothes. 'I'll tear his eyes out and make the asshole eat them!'

'Son of a bitch near crippled me!' the commander squeaked painfully. 'I'll cut his balls off and he can eat them as well!'

Flashlights at full beam the vengeance seeking duo set off in hot pursuit, going more on the sound of a stumbling and staggering quarry than anything else as the moon had disappeared completely behind some clouds plunging the rough track into inky blackness. Only when they crested the rise did the distant floodlights surrounding the Polaris base and ship provide a little more light and they were able to see their quarry some distance ahead as he plunged down into deeper darkness, fear giving him wings and carrying him over heather and hillside towards the faint lights of Daft Doug's farmhouse.

Soon Smythe Smith saw a darker shadow ahead and stumbled to a halt against the rough wall of one of the far buildings. His legs began to weaken and his breath came in ragged painful gasps. His hands shook as he felt his way along the wall pressing deeper into the shadows.

'Got to get away from here!' he thought wildly. 'Can't go into the farm, or those murdering Mafia will wipe out some poor old farming couple and their children!'

He looked frantically around and whimpered in fear when he saw the two pursuing lights bobbing down the hillside towards him and his moment of benevolent courage gave out. He staggered from the wall and into the dimly lit farmyard seeking refuge wherever he could find it, regardless of consequences.

'In the yard there!' yelled the commander as he saw a shadow move across the dim lights. 'Circle around and we'll get the son of a bitch this time!'

The riled seaman needed no further encouragement and headed swiftly towards the yard, going left round some tumbled outbuildings as the commander moved in from the right. The moon had ducked back out from the clouds and Smythe Smith saw the shadows split up and begin to cut him off. He stood confused for a moment then lurched into a shadow as he saw he was being trapped. Then he tried to shout for help, failing miserably, his throat hot and dry from fear and exhaustion.

It was nearly midnight, and suddenly the faint sound of whirring and clicking machinery began.

On the hour it got louder, much louder, leading to a crashing bedlam of bells, gongs, claxons, whistles and chimes filling the farmyard with a deafening destructive clamour of noise.

Stunned, all three men staggered about holding their ears, totally disoriented by the incredible chorus of hundreds and maybe even thousands, of clocks striking the midnight hour, all multiplied by twelve. Then the farm animals joined in, the bulls bellowed, the pigs squealed, the dogs barked, and the cocks crowed out of time.

Above the din a thin scream could be heard, building in force until it almost dominated the din. Smythe Smith had at last found his voice, even if he was now rapidly losing his sanity.

Remarkably this scream must have been heard above what in that madhouse was considered normal, for the farmhouse door burst open, adding to the din, and sending a beam of light across the yard spotlighting the two Americans and the Englishman beyond.

'Bloody thieves in the night!' roared Daft Doug, throwing his double barrelled shotgun to his shoulder and loosing a random blast across the yard. 'Ye'll no get ma wee clocks, ye thievin' rogues!'

He took more careful aim at the frantic figures and all three sprang away and headed for the back wall of the yard. The second shot blast roared out as they scrambled over the broken down wall, helping them on their way.

Before Daft Doug could reload the gun they were gone, through the tumbled pens and outhouses and into the darkness beyond, the Americans running for the hillside and Fiddin, the customs man stumbling through the cold waters of the burn and onwards for a shivering journey back to Greenock.

The last of the clocks chimed out, the last disturbed animal gave a baleful squeal, and Daft Doug slammed shut his door in triumphant salute. Then silence descended once more over the Highland hillside.

Chapter 6

A very miserable Smythe Smith sat sniffling at his desk the next morning, suffering from lack of sleep and the torturous beginnings of a cold.

'Did you check out all those long distance calls from Fiddin?' he demanded of the young custom's officer sitting opposite.

'Did that super,' Tinkle Bell replied. 'Only half a dozen regular callers over the last couple of months, and none of them of much interest to us.' He went back to the racing section of his newspaper finding that of a lot more interest than any conversation with his superior officer could be.

'Put that bloody paper down and make a proper report!' Smythe Smith roared angrily. 'I'll decide what's important and what's not!'

Reluctantly Tinkle slowly folded the paper and laid it aside; making sure the racing section was still on display. He then produced a dog-eared notebook and proceeded to flip through it with slow deliberate care. Not that he needed to be reminded of his sparse information, more to give him time to explain his unorthodox methods to his methodical boss.

'You have to understand super that nobody in Fiddin uses the local telephone system for anything that's private. Not if they want it to remain private, that is.'

'What's that supposed to mean?'

'Just that Mrs Menzies who runs the small manual telephone exchange for the immediate village has ears like the Kyles of Bute and a mouth as big as Fiddin Loch, and nothing, absolutely nothing at all, is sacred to her!'

Smythe Smith could not keep the indignation out of his

voice as he stared across at the other customs man. 'You mean she listens into other peoples telephone calls? The woman should be fired for that!'

'Maybe so super, but nobody in Fiddin seems to bother too much. It's a two way street, they get their calls listened to but also get the gossip of other peoples calls, plus at times a wee bonus. Everybody who lives there knows about it, and them that don't live there don't, but then if they don't know, then they don't complain.' Tinkle, pleased with his logic and the confusing effect it was having on the Englishman, continued. 'Anyhow, its fine for us for what she gets to know, we get to know, so it's a good thing all round.'

The super grimaced at this twisted piece of logic then brought up an objection. 'How do you know she's not lying to you?'

It was now Tinkle's turn to look indignant and he was quite vehement in his reply 'She's my mother's sister's mother in law! She wouldn't lie to family!'

The super caught the indignation in the man's voice and decided he would not go there. Bloody clan warfare had broken out in Scotland before over perceived family insults. 'Get on with the report then.' he said a bit more quietly.

Tinkle caught the tone and nodded then tapped a cryptically written page of his notebook. 'Yes, here we are. Bill Dugan who runs the local shop phones up a retailer in Glasgow twice a week or more to order his supplies. Nothing suspicious about that, he's been phoning the same firm for twenty years and his father for twenty before that, ever since the telephone system was installed.'

Smythe Smith shrugged. 'Agreed, but we'll keep an eye on it anyhow. All kinds of people are tempted into the drug trade by big money and shops are an excellent cover for distribution.'

Tinkle shrugged in wonderment and continued his report. 'Then there's the minister's wife. She phones her sister in Edinburgh every Monday and sometimes on other week days or Saturday, but of course, never on a Sunday. Complains about this and that and her sister complains back. She made an extra, extra long call, yesterday afternoon and had a real moan about some pervert she had come across up on the hill behind the village. Both sisters are really down on sex, music, television etc. A couple of old harpies! Met the sister a couple of years back when she was in Fiddin on holiday and ones as bad as the other, and both are as well avoided if possible.'

Sudden enlightenment came to the super and with it a vision of not one, but two screaming women on the hillside above Fiddin. He blushed furiously and angrily. 'Bloody interfering old religious extremist bitches! Nothing better to do with their time than pour out their bile over the telephone!'

Tinkle looked up quickly, startled by the unusually venomous outburst. Smythe Smith was no polite conversationalist but he did not usually attack women or the church. Not that Tinkle had much time for the minister's wife himself. 'Aye super, a sort of poison to poison call.'

The jibe was lost on the brooding Smythe Smith. 'Who else has been phoning?'

'Well, there is the little Italian cook on the Farnhead. He uses the local call-box to phone his brother in Glasgow at least once a week.'

'About what?' The super perked up a little, his suspicions about Italian Mafia coming to the fore and hopefully confirmed.

'Mostly about his knitting.' Tinkle said with a disinterested shrug.

'Knitting!' the super exclaimed, looking at Tinkle

sharply. 'Are you trying to get funny with me?'

Tinkle lifted both hands defensively. 'No! Honest, super, he knits scarves in his spare time! Mostly in football colours but also odd multi-coloured ones. He phones his brother who sends down the wool, and then his brother collects the scarves from Greenock and sells them at football matches. They seem to make a good few quid out of it as well.'

'You got all this stuff from a nosy telephonist?' the super asked suspiciously.

'Oh no, she doesn't speak Italian.'

'They speak Italian all the time?'

'Mostly, after all that's what they both are.'

'Then how the hell do you know what they talk about?' Smythe Smith asked angrily. 'You don't speak Italian, do you?'

Tinkle laughed out loud. 'Wish I did, there's a little Italian dish a local restaurant I would like to chat to some time.' He saw the super's face beginning to twist into a bit of a snarl and decided he would go no further on that theme. 'No, it's simple enough; I just asked Hector Donaldson when I saw him this morning.'

'You mean he speaks Italian?' asked an astounded customs man who didn't think anything about this investigation was simple. 'The bloody man can barely speak the Queen's English!'

'No super.' Tinkle said patiently. 'He doesn't speak Italian either. He does speak Gaelic though, but he carries the wool out when he's delivering stores to the Farnhead, and hands over the scarves to the brother when he comes back to Greenock. The brother talks all the time about Angelo's knitting being first class and his English is apparently near perfect. He's been in Glasgow for years.'

Smythe Smith finally got the message and began to fashion an idea from the confusion in his head. 'Sergeant

Donaldson told me yesterday that today is their stores day! We are going to take a very close look indeed at those scarves when they are brought back ashore this afternoon!'

Tinkle shrugged. Anything rather than sit about the office all day. 'Want me to borrow a sniffer dog from the Glasgow airport squad?' he enquired innocently.

'No bloody dogs!' roared Smythe Smith angrily. 'I want no bloody dogs near anything I do!'

On the Greenock quay Sergeant Donaldson lifted another box of stores from the small pile behind him and handed it down to his fisherman cousin. Hector stowed them neatly on a couple of pallets behind the small wheelhouse of the Dhu Mohr then stopped for a breather.

'Met young Bell this morning.' he stated with an enquiring look. 'He was asking me about the Italian cook on the Farnhead.'

'Aye,' the sergeant said with a contemptuous shake of his head. 'The superintendent has a bee in his bonnet about that ship now, and especially about yon Angelo He seems to think all Italians are Mafia dope smugglers!'

'Huh! The only dope about here is that superintendent!' scoffed Hector. 'Yon wee fella is no Mafia man! Who ever heard of member of yon Costa Naughty that spends their time knitting scarves?'

Donald ignored his cousin's mutilation of the Italian organisation's name and gave a shrug. 'Not unusual for a seaman to knit though, is it Hector? Dugal McIntosh used to crochet cushion covers when was away and sold them round the pubs when he was home on leave.'

'That would be the man you had to arrest last year for throwing the welder from Scott's shipyard into the river?'

'The same man. The welder called him a poofter when he brought his cushion covers into the Shipwrights Arms to show to the manager's wife. He will not be out of jail till next month.'

'That sentence he got was a bit steep was it not? I mean, just for throwing the man in the river and he was hardly in there for ten minutes till they hauled him out. It sobered the welder up though!'

Donald shrugged. 'I suppose the judge just though it a bit much that Dugal broke both the man's arms and his nose before throwing him in. They tend not to like that kind of thing.'

'Still,' observed Hector. 'Dugal was severely provoked. I wonder if he's still doing his crochet work in jail?'

The two men went back to work and soon finished loading the stores, signed the receipt for the chandler's delivery man, and cast off and headed across the river to Loch Fiddin.

A furtive figure crept out from a vantage point as soon as they departed and intercepted the chandler's truck at the dock gate. Elton Padowski was once more on the prowl for information.

'Hey buddy! Hold on a minute.' he shouted to the driver.

The truck pulled up sharply to avoid getting blood all over its tyres. 'What the hell do you want?' asked the rather tough looking driver, pointedly spitting out the open side window onto the dockside. 'You got some sort of problem with living?'

'Where are all the stores off to on that boat?' Padowski asked.

'What's it to you, Yank?' asked the driver, a suspicious grinding edge to his voice.

Padowski gave a knowing sigh. He'd met the type before. Ask him a question and they were sure to answer with a question. He had to get a proper answer though or no more night passes from the commander. Reluctantly he pulled his wallet from his pocket.

'About five pounds worth is what it is to me.' he said, pulling out a note and proffering it to the driver.

The driver grinned and whipped the note away and tucked it into his shirt pocket. 'Ta mate. No secret anyhow. I do this run every week. It's a few stores and some spare gear for a ship that's laid up in Loch Fiddin. Called the Farnhead.'

'You know the men on the fishing boat?'

'The usual fella is Hector Donaldson, but the other guy I don't know. Still, him being there saved me a bit of humping.'

The driver restarted his engine. 'Got to be going now. Time and tide and all that.'

Padowski had picked up about half the information through the accent and the slang and wanted more, but the driver obviously felt he had given enough for a fiver and rammed the truck into gear, leaving Elton chocking in the exhaust fumes. As he watched the truck disappearing round a corner Padowski didn't think he had got enough for what was probably like a day's wages for the driver. For that matter it was a day's wages for him and he just hoped that the commander would reimburse him for it. He sighed at that for he doubted it, and then brightened up. It was early yet. 'I've got the morning still!' he exclaimed and hurried out of the docks and up the hill to Hot Helen and her still warm bed.

Lewis Clarke was balefully staring at his third cup of coffee when Padowski phoned to make his report. His mood was sullen and not improved by the pile of anti-nuclear crank mail recently delivered to his cabin. He listened to the highly embroidered but still sparse details of that morning's spying mission, decided it was a bad day all round, but grasped at the only seemingly significant detail.

'Fiddin again!' he exclaimed. 'That goddamn place seems to hold quite an attraction for all kinds of weirdoes!'

'It's the ship that's laid up in the loch they're heading for, Commander.' explained Padowski. 'Not the village itself.'

Lewis Clarke ignored the difference and began to think the day might not be entirely wasted, then put his plan to Padowski. 'You got no chance of getting over there in time to see what those guys are up to at the ship, but get over to Fiddin anyhow.'

'Well sir, I've just missed the ferry,' Padowski squeaked as Hot Helen's warm body cuddled up to his. 'It might be some time before I get over there.'

The commander had not missed the change in tone, nor the second set of breathing going on over the phone, and it did not help his temper. 'Get your fat fanny over there, Padowski! Even if you have to learn to walk on water!'

The sharply rebuked seaman pulled the phone away quickly as Hot Helen's tongue started to wander round his ear. Without doubt the commander was in a foul mood this morning and any further hints that Padowski had returned to bed with his paramour would not go down well. He was quite shocked then when Lewis Clarke's voice changed and took on an almost conciliatory note. Almost, but not quite. More like a downright sneaky note, but the seaman was too astounded to notice.

'I got another idea.' added the commander. 'Why don't you take your girlfriend with you? Nobody would suspect a courting couple.'

His voice changed back to its normal command tone. 'You hear that, Padowski? Just do that!'

Padowski had his own thoughts on this and quickly expressed them. 'It wouldn't be dangerous, would it sir? I wouldn't like to take her anywhere that's dangerous.'

Lewis Clarke had his own ideas about Fiddin, but Padowski was unaware of the commander's previous night's encounter with certain gun totting mad Highlanders, nor was he likely to be told of them. Still, the man had to be reassured. 'Dangerous?' he scoffed. 'You've been reading too many cheap spy novels! This is Scotland. The Jocks don't carry guns nor run around with poison tipped umbrellas. It's a nice little village and the biggest danger you are likely to face are a bunch of goddamn flower children! Just remember not to tell your girlfriend what you are up to. Women have got big mouths and we don't want her blabbing it about that we are on to a nest of commies!'

'Wouldn't dream of it sir!' assured the seaman. He quickly hung up before the commander changed his mind, rolled over in bed, and proceeded to tell Hot Helen all about his secret and daring spy mission.

The Dhu Mohr slid alongside the sheer steel cliff of the giant bulk carrier and quickly made fast on the mooring ropes provided from above.

'Good morning, Hector' shouted down Colin Cameron. 'I see you've brought some help with you today.'

'I have that, Mr Cameron.' Hector shouted back. 'Many hands make work no bother at all, as the saying possibly goes.'

Within minutes the first pallet of stores were swinging aboard the Farnhead, David Michael driving the stores crane with practised ease while Colin, Angelo and Michael David guided it onto deck and quickly unloaded it. Within minutes the second pallet appeared above the ships bulwarks, carrying the two men from the boat as extra cargo.'

'Why, its Sergeant Donaldson is it not?' asked the surprised chief engineer, who had not recognised the burly figure from a distance in his tattered fisherman's disguise. 'I hope this visit is not for any official purpose?'

'Not at all sir.' replied the sergeant. 'I'm only giving Hector here a wee hand then we are going off for a spot of fishing.'

Colin nodded happily. 'In that case, why don't you come up to my cabin for a wee dram? Unless you consider it too early in the day?'

'Never too early for a dram, Colin, You're just like your father in that respect. He always had a dram ready for anyone visiting his fishing boat.'

The crowd quickly emptied the pallet and it was swung out ready to be lowered when the visitors were ready to go. 'Well come along then Sergeant,' Colin said, and then turned to Hector. 'The Old Man is up in his cabin waiting to sign your receipts and he wants to talk to you about taking him down to Largs next week. When you're finished, come down to my cabin for a snifter.'

Hector swung his eyes to the heavens being quite sure what kind of state the captain would be in, but followed the other two towards the chief's cabin then continued up another stair to the captain's deck. He hoped for a quick conclusion to his business, even though no doubt he would be offered a couple of drinks by the captain. That was all very fine, but he had never felt comfortable drinking whisky with a man, especially an Englishman, who put ice in a fine malt, and was even known to desecrate it with lemonade!

The chief showed the sergeant to a seat, poured his guest a generous measure of unfortunately duty paid whisky, then came swiftly to the point.

'I've known you since I was a boy, Sergeant Donaldson, and in all those years I have never heard of you, let alone seen you, picking up a fishing rod, or showing the slightest interest in doing so. Now maybe you've changed suddenly, or maybe it's none of my business, but I think there is more to you being here today than just a wish to have a wee trip on the loch!'

'Ach Colin!' exclaimed the sergeant. 'You are not fooled one wee bit, are you? It is not a big secret that I can't be telling you, but I do not want to be saying too much with all your lads about.'

'Well you'd better be saying quickly sergeant, before Hector comes back down.'

'That does not really matter for he knows damn near everything that is going on. In fact, I'm sure he knows a lot more than me about anything that goes on this side of the Firth of Clyde. He was telling me on the way across about you meeting young Jimmy Thomson in the village yesterday morning, and in a way, that is what led me to be here today.'

The sergeant quickly briefed Colin on the special squad's surveillance of the loch and Smythe Smith's suspicions.

'So you see, Colin,' he ended. 'That daft Englishman has us all chasing around every obscure back alley of suspicion, and even thinks your wee cook is a big time Mafia smuggler!'

'Angelo!' exclaimed Colin. 'That wee fella doesn't even drink and turns his nose up every time anyone lights a cigarette near him. He says the smoke makes his wool smell!'

'Aye well, Hector was telling me that he knits. Anyhow, I thought I would be warning you about the strange goings on. That daft Sassenach is capable of any sort of lunacy.'

'Thanks for the tip, sergeant. I'll keep an eye open for him.'

'You will not be saying too much about this, will you?' the sergeant asked cautiously. 'I am only a few months away from retirement and would not be wanting to get into any bother at this stage.'

'Don't worry about that, sergeant.' Colin replied. I'll be sure to keep it quiet. Now why don't you have another dram?'

As he poured himself and the sergeant another whisky there was a hard knock on the cabin door and Hector let himself in. Colin quickly poured another glass and handed it to the old fisherman. 'All your business with the Old Man completed?' he asked.

Hector acknowledged the whisky and the enquiry and shook his head in near bewilderment. 'Yon captain of yours, Colin, if you do not mind me saying so, is not right in the head! He wants me to run him all the way down to Largs next week to watch a cricket match!' He looked across at the sergeant. 'I do not expect your Englishman will be too pleased at loosing the boat for the day but I do have to look after my old customers.'

'Then we will not tell him unless we have to.' replied the sergeant with a conspiratorial grin. He raised a querulous eyebrow at Colin. 'What's so important about this cricket match that your captain would be going ashore for it? From what I hear, apart from his leave periods, he has hardly stepped on dry land since the boat was laid up.'

'I think only twice.' replied Colin with a smile. 'And that was when we ran out of whisky! As for the match, it's his old school team up here for a visit and they are playing a Royal Navy team, so he has an interest in both sides.'

'It is still a long way to go for something like cricket!' scoffed Hector. 'Now if it was sport he was interested in, he could always go to Braehead to watch the shinty, or even across to Greenock to see the football on Saturday.'

'Watching the Greenock Morton play these days is not sport!' exclaimed the sergeant bitterly. 'The way that lot are playing, it is self punishment!'

'It's not that bad.' insisted the Chief. 'They did get a

draw with Forfar last week, and were a bit unlucky not to win.'

'Against Forfar!' scoffed the policeman, who took his football very seriously. 'Those laddies are only bridie makers! Not real footballers!'

Hector knew well his cousin's attitude to the national game and could see that the conversation was leading into a prolonged vivisection of every football match that had taken place in Scotland during the entire season, its fair points, its fouls, and inevitably it would waste an otherwise tranquil day. Having the privileges of a frequent visitor to Colin's cabin he helped himself to another whisky and attempted to change the subject.

'I see your terrible twins have got their submarine launched.'

'More an underwater chariot.' corrected Colin. 'And apart from a few minor snags it seems to be performing well.'

'That funny looking pile of junk by the gangway is a submarine?' asked the astonished sergeant.

'That's probably a good way to describe it.' Colin agreed. 'The twins have this idea of searching for the Bonnie Prince's treasure in Loch Fiddin, rather than Loch Garnock.'

'They might as well.' said the sergeant. 'Every diver in the last hundred years or so has scoured Loch Garnock for that treasure, and without as much as turning up a bent tin brooch! The Yankee Navy practically scrubbed the loch bed clean before they moved in and have hoovered it regularly since they did!.'

'Aye!' proclaimed Hector bitterly with his teeth clenched. 'And scared every fish out of that loch into this one in the process!'

'All to my advantage.' Colin said cheerfully. 'The fishing up here is grand now!'

'But why the submarine?' asked the sergeant. 'Garnock is deeper but even then everybody else has only used scuba diving from a boat. It is not as if the loch is all that deep, no more than sixty feet or so, a couple of wetsuits and they would be ready to go.'

'They've got the suits right enough.' Colin said. 'And have been using them since they were children, and they need them for the sub as they will only be sitting on top of it, not inside. But Fiddin is not like Garnock which is fairly clear; here the River Fid brings down a lot of black peaty water and makes the loch pretty murky. The submarine is only a carriage to carry some big sealed batteries and a powerful set of underwater lights. Without them it would take forever to search the loch bottom.'

'Still seems a lot of work to look for a treasure which is probably not there.' argued the sergeant, his professional curiosity aroused.

'The lads have a fair bit of free time on their hands.' Colin replied. 'Besides, they hope to take the sub down to the Mediterranean when they go on a long leave, and hire it out there to tourists. They have done a few test dives in the shallows yesterday and hope to do a night dive this evening at high water. I'm not too keen on that but they do seem to know what they are doing and, besides, I can't really stop them without being dismissed as an old fuddy-duddy!'

'They will soon be stopping if they come face to face with the Fiddin Monster!' warned Hector, his brows beetled and wary.

'You and your monster!' scolded Colin. 'You've even got Angelo believing in that beast!'

'There is bad luck in the loch!' Hector exclaimed quite seriously. 'You will not be catching me dropping my nets in it no matter how good the fishing is! And for sure, there are not many around here who would be taking that risk either!' He waved a warning finger at Colin. 'Your own father would not as much as drop a line in Fiddin and he was not a man to be afraid of anything!'

'I doubt if my little fishing line is going to annoy your monster, Hector.'

'Maybe not, but your twins buzzing around in their wee electric boat might get it really annoyed! And who is to say what it might do then?'

Hector reached out for the whisky bottle again but the sergeant waved an admonishing finger at him. 'We had better be going, Hector. I'm sure Mr Cameron has work to do, and we have as well, even if it does seem a bit pointless.'

The fisherman reluctantly withdrew his hand. 'Aye, I suppose that is true enough, a pity though, as it's a nice drop of whisky.'

He turned and shook hands with Colin 'Many thanks for the dram or two, Mister Cameron. I will be seeing you again a few days time when I collect your captain.' The fisherman shook his head in resignation. 'You had better be reminding the man of it when the time comes, for I am not too sure he knows what day of the week it is!'

'I'll do that Hector' Colin replied. 'Though it's so peaceful around here, with one day much like the other, that I'm not always sure what day it is myself!'

Chapter 7

The Dhu Mohr pulled away from the steel walls of the bulk carrier and made its way south through the dark still water, the Farnhead's crew waving farewell from the deck, while the captain, glass in hand, wondering what a fishing boat had been doing alongside his ship, prepared for another hard day's work in his cabin. There had been a lot of days like that, and he at times puzzled over why he seemed to get so little done after so much time spent on it. Not for a moment did he suspect it had something to do with the glass in his hand which he now went inside to refill.

The small fishing boat chugged away towards the wide deep channel in the Clyde and Hector handed over the wheel to his cousin and started to prepare a cup of tea.

'What was it that young Bell was pointing out to you in the newspaper earlier on?' he asked.

'It was an article about that Member of Parliament of ours, the bloody honourable Hugh Hogarth, blabbing his mouth off about the police force!' the sergeant replied. He slipped the newspaper from his coat pocket and handed it to Hector. 'See for yourself, it is right at the top of page two.'

The fisherman opened the paper and clicked his tongue a few times. 'By god, Donald, that lass here has a fine chest on her! It is a wonder she can stand upright with all that weight pulling her forward.' He switched his eyes to the less compelling page opposite. 'Aye, here it is about the police. There is even a picture of that daft man himself and, going by it I would say our man in the Westminster gabble house would have a bit of difficulty staying upright himself, though his centre of gravity is a bit further down. Mind you he has a fair bit of weight further up as well, that nose on him as big as the bulbous bow on a red painted ocean liner.'

'Far too big!' stated Donald emphatically. 'He is so anxious to hold onto his tiny majority he will do anything just to get his name in the papers, like last year sprouting like a big wart from the top of a tank turret hatch, though that backfired a bit when it took two hours to push and pull the silly bugger back out. Nowadays though it is some daft campaign or another and the latest is to annoy the police force.'

'Says here that he is wanting a special task force set up to look for hooligans and vandals. I would have thought that Greenock had enough of them without looking for any more!'

'He got his special task force set up to look for drug smugglers, and much good has that done!' exclaimed Donald sarcastically. 'No doubt his hooligan task force will give the Chief Constable a chance to get rid of a few misfits for a while.'

'As long as they are not silly enough to put an Englishman in charge!' stated Hector. 'By the way, you never did tell me what young Bell and Jimmy Thomson did to get pushed into a detail like this. Mind you, if it is a secret, I will not be asking you.'

Donald shrugged his indifference. 'No secret really. Not in the town anyway, though if anyone tried to put it in print there would be a few blunt denials all round. It was a direct result of Hogarth's interfering that got the two of them in trouble.'

'Sticking that elephant's trunk of a nose in, was it?' Hector asked.

'It was in a way,' Donald replied with a hint of a smile.

'Though it was the other end of him that took the punishment!' Donald took his tea from Hector and handed the wheel over to the fisherman who was totally at home steering single handed. 'You see, young Bell was the perpetrator of a wee practical joke that misfired. He knew a colleague of his was going out one morning in the customs launch to clear a ship that was at anchor at the Tail off the Bank, so he spread some rather powerful contact adhesive on the passenger seats. So he would stick to the job, as it were. Unfortunately, or maybe fortunately, depending on how you look at it, that was the very morning that the honourable Hugh turned up with a senior customs official from through Edinburgh way, them both wanting a waterfront tour of the fair town of Greenock. They took the two available seats and set out with the boarding officer standing and Jimmy Thomson, who was driving the boat at the time. To cut the story short, when they returned, it took the pair of them some time to wiggle their way out of their trousers, Hogarth leaving behind a fair bit of skin in the process as his were much thinner than the other mans!'

Hector was grinning like a Cheshire Cat. 'I would dearly have wished to have seen that!'

'Well a few did without realising what was going on! Then in borrowed dungarees they had to make their way up through the port to where Hogarth left his car. The fat MP was recognised by a few people who speculated why he was limping his way about the town in tatty old dungarees, but nobody had any hard evidence as Jimmy Thomson and the boarding officer were sworn to silence. Still, young Bell was suspected and took this daft job to get away from pointing fingers while Jimmy got it in the ear for just being in charge of the boat at the time!'

Hector's grin had now turned to open laughter as he imagined the scene. 'I can see that he would not be too happy if the newspapers got a hold of such a story, never mind the possibility of a few photographs of him wriggling out of his pants! Mind you, for a man who is very shaky in his Parliamentary seat, it did give him a seat for a while which was very solid and immovable!'

Donald had swung he boat round as he finished his story and they were now well clear of Loch Fiddin and cutting west to Loch Garnock. He pointed across the river towards the fast approaching Fiddin ferry.

'Here comes Angus Kerr, right on time, or at least not more than twenty minutes late.'

The Dhu Mohr ran down the side of the ferry, the skippers shouting hurried greetings across the foaming waters between them, then the fishing boat bobbed through the ferry wake and headed towards the American base. On the ferry, Angus Kerr gave them a parting blast on the whistle then continued towards the slipway at Garnock Point to discharge his cargo of three cars and two closely hugging foot passengers.

'Oh my, Elton, isn't that dangerous, that little boat coming as close to the ferry as that?' asked the hugging and huggable Hot Helen.

'Shucks honey, that's really nothing! When we go on manoeuvres we got thousand foot long battleships running along inches apart.' exaggerated the daring Padowski, who had never actually seen a battleship and who's only ocean voyage had been a best forgotten nightmare journey across the Atlantic on the bobbing and rolling base ship.

'Oh Elton, you sailors are really brave!' exclaimed Hot Helen, unaware of Padowski's absolute terror of deep water. 'It makes me feel really safe when I'm along with you, no matter how many spies are about.'

Padowski puffed out his chest and held the girl closer. The response was very encouraging, but cut short a s the ferry ground itself onto the concrete shore ramp nearly tumbling the distracted lovers onto the deck. Elton glared up at the bridge, but the skipper grinned back, having timed his berthing to perfection. It was not his fault if his passengers were too busy to watch where the ferry was going. He lowered the ramp and watched as the couple stepped ashore and made their way up to the waiting local bus for the short run into the village.

'We'll get some chow in the local bar, and then go for a walk in the heather.' said the American seaman to Helen. 'Remember, just act natural and we won't arouse any suspicion.'

Hot Helen eyed the seaman's holdall where he had thoughtfully stowed a large woolly blanket. 'Oh Elton, let's find somewhere up the hill that's very quiet, then I'll really act natural!'

Padowski leered back and gave Hot Helen another anticipatory hug.

The Londoners Arms was never the busiest of pubs at any time, for if the entire drinking population of Fiddin arrived at the door simultaneously there would still have been room for a couple of wayward stragglers. As it was, the only locals in sight that lunchtime were virtually a permanent feature, as was their noisy and usually inconclusive game of dominos.

Elton and his clinging girlfriend were ushered in by the bus driver who never failed to guide tourists in the direction of the pub, on the theory that his consideration would often be rewarded with the offer of a dram. His diligence once more met with success, Elton eagerly paying for the man's drink in the hope of extracting some information for his pressing commander. Unfortunately for Elton though, the driver's drink was served and downed in one practised gulp, and the driver was hurrying out the door before Elton had even time to open a conversation, and long before his and Helen's drinks were served.

'The bus will be waiting.' muttered the driver in apology for his hurried departure. What exactly it would be waiting for, apart from the driver, Elton was none too sure, for it was obvious no passengers were making the return trip.

Helen skimmed through the surprisingly good lunch menu and made her choice, Elton automatically ordering hamburger and French fries for himself. He felt safer sticking to what he knew, having at one time found himself staring at a rather revolting looking brown mass called "Haggis", and a pile of yellow fibrous material called "Neeps". He did force himself to eat it, the occasion demanding some diplomacy, and found it fairly palatable, but had been stupid enough later to enquire of its exact nature, and had no desire to repeat the experiment. Besides, he remembered having to rush away to dispose of his stomach's contents after hearing that it was a sheep's stomach that had held his meal's contents.

He looked around for a place to sit. The domino players rattled on at one table, another whole corner was occupied by a browned bunch of hikers and their assorted travelling equipment, and the only remaining table by two inebriated fishermen discussing such exotic faraway ports such as Ardrossan, Ayr and Oban.

Seeing his look the barman nodded towards a door at the side. 'Just you and your young lady be going through the side room. The food will be taking about ten minutes and I will be getting the wife to set you a place through there. It is much quieter, with only the minister in there reading his paper, and he is such a quiet wee man that would not be disturbing anybody.'

Padowski thanked the man and carried the drinks through to a pleasant little room with a big picture window looking out onto the loch, finding himself and Helen a place by an ornate unlit fireplace. The small bespectacled figure of the minister looked up from his newspaper, sipped briefly from a half pint glass, and then gave the newcomers a smile and a quiet greeting. The seaman beamed back. Here was the very man who would know about everything that happened in the village. He nudged Hot Helen, who caught his quick conspiratorial glance and gave the minister one of her special smiles, a smile which would have encouraged even a saint into conversational indiscretion.

Mr MacIvar, more used to his thankfully absent wife's grim forbidding scowl, smiled happily back. Padowski slipped into an interrogation with unexpected ease.

'Say, reverend, is that your cute little church up on the hill there?' he asked.

The minister laid aside his nearly finished newspaper, which he customarily only held onto long enough as an innocent excuse to sit quietly sipping his drink. 'Not exactly mine.' He replied in a friendly jesting manner. 'Though I am sure the Lord would not object too much to my assuming its ownership, having looked after it for the last twenty-five years.'

Helen gave a little giggle. 'It's a lovely little church. Is it possible to have a look inside it?'

'Without a doubt.' replied the minister with a little bit of pride. 'It's not your Glasgow Cathedral by any means. But the woodwork inside is very good and all done by local craftsmen over the last four hundred years. And on a fine day like this with the sun coming through the stained glass windows, it really is a pretty sight.'

'Is it open at a special time?' Helen asked.

The minister gave an amused chuckle. 'Up here we are not too bothered by thieves or vandals, so the door of the Lord's house is always open. Especially to a pretty girl like you.' he added impishly, earning a genuine special smile from Helen.

He thought suddenly of his stern wife, no doubt preparing his lunch, which was served at precisely the same time every day, in the same solemn manner, and gave a regretful sigh. 'I'm afraid I have a previous appointment or I would have been happy to show you around, but,' and he glanced at the pair knowingly. 'I expect you will prefer your own company and will find your way about the place.'

Elton tried to get his own agenda back on track. 'We were going for a walk up past the church to the hilltop.' he said. 'It's not private land, is it?'

'Not at all. The whole hillside was given to the church about two hundred years ago by the Duke of Argyle, to be used as a graveyard for the villagers. He must have been expecting a powerful lot of dying to be going on, for, as you will see, the present graveyard barely covers a tenth of the acreage available.'

'Anyone famous buried there.' Elton asked.

'Not really.' the minister replied. 'You'll see one fancy big stone though which marks the last resting place of the last Laird of Fiddin who died in nineteen thirty. Ate and drank himself to death, I heard. He was a huge man of thirty odd stone they say, and it was a terrible wet day they picked to bury him and the path up to the graveyard was very slippery. There is a small stone besides the Laird's belonging to one of the pallbearers.The poor man slipped on the mud, fell down the hillside and had his neck broken when the coffin fell on him!'

The couple sat there enthralled by the minister's tragic story which was interrupted by the barkeep's wife who came through to lay out their cutlery, and then he carried on.

'Ever since then the people of Fiddin will only bury their loved ones if it has been dry for a couple of days, and in winter, that can mean waiting a long time. As a result we often send the bodies over to the crematorium in Greenock. Ashes are much more portable.'

Elton turned to Helen when the minister had concluded. 'Honey, I gotta see this place. It sounds real historical.'

'Anything you like, Elton.' her eyes twinkled. 'It sounds a real restful place.'

The minister, misinterpreting Helen's words, tried a small sales pitch. 'A lovely place to be laid to rest. It may sound a bit premature, but I could sell you a plot very cheaply. A sort of investment in the future, as it were, though I would hope, the very distant future!'

Helen laughed out loudly. 'Oh, Mr MacIvar, you're surely pulling our legs!' She paused for a moment of thought. 'There is something else though we might be interested in. We might just use your little church for a wedding!'

Elton looked stunned and gave a small gasp, while Helen gave him a "don't you dare contradict me!" look, then turned her sweet smile back to the minister who smiled like it was Christmas.

'My pleasure, my dear! We have not had a wedding in the village for over five years! Alas, the young people around her move away to the bright lights of the big cities and we seldom even hear about them getting married till long after the event. Have you set a date yet?' he asked Elton.

'No, no, not yet!' stumbled the totally confused seaman. He did like Helen but----. He looked at her face and saw a cold shadow pass over it and then an equally cold shiver ran down his spine. 'I suspect we'll get engaged very soon though!' he hurriedly added before a knife joined the cold shiver.

Helen smiled warmly again and hugged the trapped seaman. To her, a promise made in the presence of a man of the cloth was nearly as good as a fully witnessed marriage ceremony and could always be thrown down on the bench of a court of law.

The minister smiled his acknowledgement of the pact, then looked at his watch and gave a little frown. For the first time in years he would be late for his lunch, no doubt putting his wife into a particularly bad mood for the rest of the day. Still, it would be worth it if this wedding came off.

'I will have to be going now.' he apologised sadly as he quickly finished his drink. 'You must let me know well in advance what your plans are, and I will make sure you have the finest wedding this area has ever seen for many a day!'

He shook hands with the almost engaged couple and left, depositing his borrowed paper and the empty glass on the bar outside, before almost skipping away along the street. Elton breathed a sigh of relief. He was in deep enough trouble after a ten minute chat with this "quiet wee man that would not be disturbing anybody." Another ten minutes and Helen would probably have had this pub arranged for the reception and talking to the minister about christening arrangements for their first couple of kids!

The meals arrived just then and he was saved from further incriminating conversation with his fiancée to be. Better to keep his mouth shut except to shovel food in, while his brain turned over the implications of this day's dangerous work. It was not till several minutes later, while opening his mouth briefly to cramming a forkful of hamburger a la Fiddin, that he realised, in ten minutes of conversation with the man he expected to know everything, he had learned absolutely nothing of the slightest interest to his issuer of shore passes, the contents of the local graveyard hardly likely to placate the vengeful ire of Commander Barnaby Lewis Clarke.

The very boat which was of the utmost interest to the Commander, was at that moment anchored off the American jetty in Loch Garnock, its two occupants watching the latest posse of American seamen on their way ashore.

'Yon big darkie fella seems to be a frequent visitor ashore, is he not Donald?' asked the boat's owner.

'He is that, Hector, though I would be having some doubts if he will be carrying any drugs with him.'

'I would not be too sure about that, Donald. He is a big villainous looking man, and definitely has the criminal look about him.'

'Yes he does, so I did some checking up on him a few days ago, and in his case, looks are very deceiving! It turned out he is the ship's chaplain and spends a lot of time ashore doing charity work and giving religious lessons to local groups.'

'Well I never!' exclaimed the surprised fisherman. 'And to think that only a few years ago we were sending missionaries for him and his friends to eat!' He paused for a moment as an idea struck him. 'Do you suppose that superintendent of yours would be willing to go to Africa as a missionary, him being a bit plump and probably tender as well?'

The sergeant had a quick mental vision of Smythe Smith sitting in a big bubbling stew pot surrounded by hungry looking chanting natives. He gave a small regretful sigh. 'If it could only be, Hector, but I am afraid the man might prove to be unpalatable to even the hungriest of natives. He is likely to be a bit on the sour side!'

The two men sat in silence for a few minutes contemplating the soft heather clad purple hills sweeping down to the clear deep waters of the loch. Hector was thinking of what these waters might conceal, or more specifically, what the waters of the neighbouring loch might conceal. 'Would you be thinking, Donald, that all this time people have been looking in the wrong place for Prince Charlie's treasure?'

His cousin gave a non-committal shrug. 'Most people spend most of their life looking in the wrong place for what they think they want, and very few find it. For those that do not, it seems to do little harm.'

'Those Taffy twins might just be the lads to find what they are looking for. I have had a few chats with them in the past and they are clever boys, though it's very hard to tell who is who.'

'I do not think it really matters, Hector. When you are talking to twins I think you are talking to only one person who has had the luck, or bad luck maybe, to have two bodies to see them through the wear and tear of life.' He screwed up his brow in recollection, 'I met twin sisters in Glasgow many years ago when I was in the police force there. A couple of really braw lassies and as like as two peas in a pod! You spoke to one it was like speaking to the other even though they might have been miles apart. I swear those lassies were telepathic! I used to take them out, to the pictures and the dancing, and what not, and for all I know, maybe it was both of them I was taking out at the one time, or maybe it was both of them I was taking out at different times!'

'My word!' exclaimed Hector. 'It must have been a difficult situation for you. I suppose though if those lassies were that tele thing you mentioned; it would at least save them a few shillings in telephone bills.'

'Probably, Hector, and you are right about it proving difficult. One of them though, had a bad case of sticky fingers, and one day near emptied half the stores in Sauchiehall Street before they caught her. Then the daft buggars let her go on bail without taking fingerprints or anything. Before you know it, they had got their lovely little twin heads together and both were swearing in court that they were the one who had been caught shoplifting.'

Hector looked startled at that. 'Are you sure the other had not been involved anyway, them being so alike?'

'Perhaps she had in the past, but not that day, for she was along with me on a day trip to Rothesay and Millport. It was a fine day for a sail "Doon the Water" as well, and I was thinking of proposing to her that evening coming back up past Dumbarton Rock. But then, one of those big daft sea gulls dropped a great splatter on a bald man's head and we all fell about laughing and the moment was lost forever!'

The policeman gave a long, and perhaps, regretful, sigh. 'The next time I saw her she was up in dock with her sister though neither would even say who was who and I had no idea which one I was almost engaged to.'

Hector nodded in sympathy. 'And how did the sheriff deal with it if he did not know which one was guilty?'

'He was quite fair about it, really. He told them he had been intending to give the guilty party a six month sentence, but he would ignore that seeing he could not afford to send the innocent party to jail, so instead, because both were conspiring against the court, he would give each of them three months in jail for contempt of court! I never saw them again after that for as soon as they got out they were away to England or some other foreign parts, and are no doubt bamboozling other poor souls there!'

'Ach, Donald, I have no doubt it was all for the best in the long run. Twins are definitely twice the trouble!' Hector shook his head and returned to the original subject of the conversation. 'Do you think these Welsh laddies have any chance of finding the treasure in Loch Fiddin?'

The sergeant laughed. 'I am surprised you still believe

in that story.' he replied. 'I personally think it is a load of romantic nonsense.'

'Do not laugh at me, Donald Donaldson!' Hector stated with a wag of his finger. 'You never believed in the monster either, but that poor soul they dragged out the loch four years ago had been half eaten by it!'

'Or half chewed up by some boat's propeller, more likely!' The sergeant pointed over at the American base ship. 'There are a dozen or more boats over there belonging to them fellas that zip about all over the place without regard to rules and regulations and at all times of the day and night. Even their captain has got himself a brand new one to run about in and disturb the fish.'

'And that is what us being out here pretending to fish makes us look all the dafter!' Hector pointed out. 'Every man with a bit of sense within a hundred miles of here knows that there are no fish left in this loch!'

'And who says those Yanks have any sense at all?' asked his cousin.

'True enough.' Hector conceded. 'There are not many about here that think they do!'

One non-sensible Yank was at that time trying to make sense out of the strange craft which had only then pulled out from the blind side of the large bulk carrier moored in the loch below. Elton Padowski's forehead creased in puzzlement as the craft silently cut through the still waters of Loch Fiddin. Silently? Padowski, though no great navigator, knew boats didn't move silently over the water without sails on a windless day. Not even with sails on a windy day. Not unless they were nuclear powered submarines and his people had the only nukes around here, and even Padowski knew that it was no nuke.

A pair of binoculars would have shown him a lot more to puzzle about as the twins took their battery powered craft southwards to the shallower part of the loch for another test dive, but without binoculars, probably fortunately for the simple seaman's near overloaded brain, he had only the problem of silence to worry about.

'They'll not be able to see us up here, will they?' asked the near naked Hot Helen who was peering over his shoulder at the puzzling craft.

'Gee, honey, there's no chance of that. Just nobody can see what we're up to here.'

'Oh good, Elton! I've never done anything like this in the open air before.' She started to drag him down into the heathery depths of the little hollow they had found after a steep climb up the hillside.

'Hang on a minute, honey, I gotta record this for the commander. He retrieved his notebook and pencil from his discarded jacket. His discarded shirt and trousers lay on top of her skirt and blouse and a blanket covered the little grassy space between the clumps of heather.

'It really is exiting being up here with you, Elton.' continued Helen breathlessly as she nibbled at his ear. 'Just like being in a James Bond movie!'

'Sure, honey.' He said distractedly, muttering away to himself as he scribbled the time in his notebook and added, "One boat left freighter and headed down the loch, two occupants visible. No sound." 'It's a pity nothing exciting is happening.' he added in reflection.

'It's just about to!' Helen cried in excitement, grabbing the seaman and pulling him down to her eagerly waiting bosom. 'It's really just about to!'

The heather swayed and tossed in the cool afternoon breeze, soft grunts and squeals coming drifting up from the lovers hollow, then Padowski's querulous voice broke through the reverie.

'Helen, honey, you got your nose in my ear, and it's all wet!'

'No it's not, Elton!'

'It is honey, and cold!'

There was a small unpunctuated silence as both thought about what was happening, and then Padowski whispered. 'Honey, is that you panting?'

He slowly turned his head. A large wet tongue wiped over his face and two large brown eyes framed a long black wet nose which poked through the heather. Elton sprung up with a horrified howl while Hot Helen gave a small strangled scream. The frightened black Labrador sprung back colliding with black stockinged legs of its astonished owner.

Mrs MacIvar stared in horror at the almost naked couple in front of her. Yesterday a Peeping Tom, today, naked heathens fornicating at her feet! She drew in an outraged breath and then let it go in a scream more of rage than horror. What next was likely to happen on her beloved hillside?

The trusty walking stick lashed out catching Padowski across his scantily clad buttocks and nearly knocking him over. 'Fornicators!' she howled. 'Filthy heathen devils!'

Elton stumbled about grabbing various items of clothing and dodging the scything walking stick as it was swung again and again, with a lot more vigour than anyone would have expected from such a small elderly woman. Hot Helen rolled helplessly down the slope in a tangled bundle of blanket and clothing, happily pursued by the Labrador which thought this melee was the best fun it had been involved in for a very long time.

'Jesus Christ, Lady.' cried Elton as the walking stick caught him right across the calf again almost knocking him over. 'Gimme a break!'

The words hardly got out of his mouth before he nearly got a broken shoulder as the stick pounded on it. Elton gave a pained scream and then the dog joined in with a howl of delight as it leapt over the tangled bundle ahead of it and started worrying the blanket round Helen.

'Take not the Lord's name in vain!' screamed the offended minister's wife as she lashed out in even more fury at Elton's misuse of the name of Jesus.

Elton managed to duck that one but stumbled as he beat a hasty retreat down the slope, fell over the struggling Hot Helen, and landed heavily on the unfortunate dog. It howled even louder, no longer amused at the melee, and then took off up the hill towards the comparative safety of its mistress's feet.

'Dog beater!' screamed Mrs. MacIvar. 'I'll teach you not to attack poor dumb animals!' She lifted the wieldy stick again, this time high over her head, the intent obvious and the result likely to be highly damaging, but her feet tangled with Helen's discarded brassiere and she fell violently onto her already half demented hound. Its howls became frantic and it wriggled free and started to run up the hill in limping confused circles. Mrs MacIvar struggled to regain her feet in the tufted heather, reciting her entire litany of curses in her native Gaelic tongue.

Elton and Hot Helen had in the meantime disentangled and, in the short respite, had almost completed dressing, though continued to retreat downhill and away from their furious assailant. She eventually regained her feet and started to set out in pursuit of the couple but was distracted by the howls of the terrified dog which gave a last frantic and choked howl before heading for the hilltop. Mrs MacIvar was in two minds now, but the hesitation meant her quarry was almost out of range, so instead gave them one more curse then turned and started stumbling up the hillside in pursuit of her crazed dog.

The retreating lovers, trailing their blanket and the few remaining clothes, hurried off in the opposite direction, pausing only briefly in surprise as the angry wild harridan who had attacked them, called frantically after her pet. 'Satan!' she cried. 'Come back to your mistress, Satan!'

Chapter 8

Commander Lewis Clarke's boss was at that moment giving him a little hell. The captain of the base ship was roaring so loud down the telephone that had Lewis Clarke put it down and stood out in the alleyway every word would still have been clearly audible. The captain was well known for his loud voice and it was always wiser to put as much distance between oneself and his vocal chords as possible, but there was no escape in this instance. The unfortunate commander had to listen, much as he did not like what was being said, as it concerned his pet hate, the bane of his present life, the dreaded Mothers against Polaris.

'You, mister!' roared the captain. 'Are supposed to keep tabs on those bitches, but one of them got into the civic reception I was at yesterday and shoved a letter in my face complaining about the lack of communication between the U.S. Navy and them! Up to me the only communication they would get is my stiff boot up their collective asses, but, there were all sorts of Limey politicians there and our Admiral as well, so I have to reply to the goddamn letter!'

The captain paused briefly for breath and Lewis Clarke cringed all the more.

'You still with me?' the captain snarled.

'Yes sir!' Clarke replied with some urgency though really with extreme reluctance.

'Well, mister, I promised a reply by fourteen hundred today, and when I promise, you deliver! You got that? I'm sending my reply down right now, so you get it and get over to that slum camp of theirs and deliver it. Personally,

Clarke, and with due apologies, so get it?'

'Yes sir.' mumbled the commander.

'I don't hear you, mister!'

'Aye, aye sir!' Lewis Clarke roared back.

'That's better, Commander, much better. Now remember, fourteen hundred on the dot I promised them! We can't make the bitches love us but we can at least show them the United States submarine service is punctual!'

The bull roar faded away and Lewis Clarke waited for the click before slamming down the telephone. The old ball breaker was at it again! Bucking for admiral's rank and using his back to climb upwards!

A few minutes later a seaman delivered the fateful sealed letter and Lewis Clarke for a moment was tempted to steam it open and peruse the contents before common sense took over. The repercussions of being caught by either sender or receiver would be murderous, and those damn women would probably have the letter forensically examined before the opened it up just in case it proved to be even the slightest little bit radioactive! The commander gritted his teeth, changed into a fresh uniform, fortified himself with a generous slug of neat Jim Beam whisky, and then headed for whatever awaited him ashore.

Forty plus wild looking women chanting "No Bomb Here!" awaited him just outside the car park perimeter fence and he wished he had taken another slug of whisky before he had come ashore, but that was one of their milder dirges. "Hang the Yanks!" was a bit further up the scale and had more vehemence in it, and "Kill the Baby Killers!" meant you should keep well clear as this was screamed in voices that only a threatened mother could possibly achieve. On days like that, approaching them was not an option as the screams were often accompanied by a hail of fist sized or larger rocks. That this appeared to be one of their quieter days, the commander was very grateful. The shear viciousness of these "Mothers" had horrified him ever since their first encounter and he still blushed at some of the appalling and very unladylike language they used, a weakness they had quickly noted and used against him at every opportunity.

He pulled the letter from his uniform jacket pocket and headed for the small group standing by the closed wire mesh gate.

'Well, if it isn't the lovely Commander Lewis Clarke!' Bella Bolnay said in mock astonishment. 'Why don't you invite me in, Lewis, and we can get to know each other better.'

Clarke cursed under his breath. It had to be her, back again to plague him, and he blushed furiously as he remembered one incident which he preferred to forget but the entire base remembered only too well. He gritted his teeth and raised his voice to its polite official level.

'Ms Bolnay, I thought we had lost you for a while.'

He sincerely hoped they had, but was of course disappointed, and also had no intention of opening the gate. The one time he had done so resulted in him losing his trousers and most of the rest of his uniform as well.

Bella grinned at him. She still had the commander's trousers and one of her followers was wearing his shirt while another had turned his jacket, complete with three sleeve rings of rank, into a fairly stylish backpack for her baby, on the theory that not even the stupidest policeman, on recognising it for what it was, wouldn't dare rip a child carrying backpack off the mother. Not if he valued his job, nor for that matter, his life.

Bella was standing there savouring that incident and smiled sweetly as she replied. 'Now Commander, you don't think I would go away and leave you brave boys up her in the wilderness alone? I've only been down south visiting some friends who are busy entertaining some air force friends of yours with their little cruise missiles. Not quite in the same class of murderers as your lot, but also worth a protest or two!'

Lewis Clarke noted how the last sentence had turned nasty and decided to get on with this onerous task. He pushed the letter through the mesh of the gate and hissed a barely audible 'Dyke Bitch!'

'Bitch indeed!' Bella screamed back with ear spitting volume, then grabbed his hand and drew his arm violently through the mesh. 'I'll give you bitch all right!' She half turned and roared to her followers. 'Now girls! For freedom and the Mothers!'

The commander's uniform jacket was grabbed by a multitude of hands and he was hauled hard against the wire and held securely there. He could only watch in horror as the women, all chanting now forgotten, produced heavy duty wire clippers and industrial sized bolt cutters and proceed to slice through fence, hinges and gate bolts. Within seconds large sections of wire toppled to the ground and the gate hinges and bolts were cut through allowing the gate to be pushed aside and a screaming mass of tool armed women charged across the car park to the two horrified marines at the guardhouse.

'Call the cops!' howled Lewis Clarke as he struggled to free himself, unassisted by the marines who only frantically sprang inside and slammed the door on the wave of women. The gate, shorn of its supports, began to topple towards Bella and the women holding him against it and they momentarily let him go. Freed, he sprang back, pushed aside a couple of grabbing girls, and leaping over car bonnets and boots, sprinted panic stricken through the car park towards the quay.

'Cast off you idiot!' he shouted at Maitland Jnr. who had been left in charge of the borrowed liberty boat.

'Don't let the bitches on the boat!'

Maitland had no intention of letting anyone on the boat and was already accelerating the powerful diesel engine. He pushed the reverse pitch lever in and the boat leapt away from the quay, quickly opening up a ten foot gap, about five feet more than the commander's flying leap could carry him! He hit the water in full flight, mouth wide open and still shouting at Maitland Jnr. and immediately swallowed a large salty quantity of Loch Garnock as he went under deeply, only just avoiding braining himself on the steel reinforced bow of the big boat.

Moments later he surfaced again, coughing and spitting, then began to sink under the weight of his soaked uniform, but was luckily, or not, stopped by Maitland Jnr. grabbing him violently by his springy hair. The Commander screamed in pain, leading to more coughing and spluttering plus a great cheer ashore, followed by a hail of rotten fruit and vegetables, carefully hoarded by the Mothers against Polaris for their occasional fairly friendly forays against the Americans. On not so friendly days the loch shore pebbles provided an almost unlimited supply of rocks and pebbles for more lethal intent.

Beyond the car park the crashing of hammers and splintering of glass bore testimony to the demonstrators attack on the guardhouse which fortunately had been built fairly sturdily with bars on the two small windows but as they women were now prising apart the very wooden sides of it, it looked like it might just fall before too long. Maitland could do little about that, he decided, and after hauling the commander aboard, backed off further out of range of the vegetarian barrage and thanked his lucky stars he had not stepped ashore.

A security patrol boat roared past towards the quay carrying four tough looking sailors and a massively built petty officer who looked like he could really handle himself, but the petty officer was not stupid and had noticed Lewis Clarkes ripped sleeve insignia as he went past. It was a very boring job cruising round the loch all day long in circles and his men had been picked for aggressiveness, so they cared not a whit whether it was male, or dubiously female, they were let loose on, but it was always better to have an officer to blame in case of repercussions. He backed his boat up till he could call across to where that scuffed up officer was divesting himself of the soaked uniform jacket.

'You want my boys to go up there and kick shit out of those crazy dames?' he asked the commander.

'Back off.' croaked Lewis Clarke, as he disentangled himself from some foul green stringy vegetable matter which was oozing round his neck. 'They can't do much damage there, but if they get a hold of your boat and get across to the base, there's no saying what havoc they can cause.'

'I reckon my boys could handle them.' shouted back the petty officer, pointing to a second patrol boat full of men sliding in towards the car park quay. He was reluctant to back off and abandon his chance of a good fight which could be turned into an epic after a few embellishments.

'It took ten marines and twenty Limey cops just to shift them off the road last month!' exclaimed the commander. 'Now back off!'

The PO shrugged his annoyance and pulled away from the quay and a sharp splintering noise followed by a big cheer attracted everybody's attention ashore. The sturdy guardhouse door had finally given way. Moments later two screaming marines, their uniforms torn to rags, were propelled along the quay by a dozen triumphant Mothers, and then thrown in the loch followed by their riot sticks and helmets.

The commander directed a patrol boat in to pick up the floundering marines, having no wish to subject himself to another stinking missile attack.

Bella Bolnay appeared at the quay side and shouted out clearly to the cringing Lewis Clarke.

'Next time we go for your nuclear warmongering ship itself!' She turned to her chanting followers and waving a meaty fist in the air began the usual chants. 'Down with Polaris! Yanks go home. No nukes here!'

They kept this up only for a couple of rounds then Bella stopped them with a determined shout. 'Now sisters, destroy their transport! Only official and senior officers cars though! We have no quarrel with the oppressed underclass!'

Lewis Clarke watched in horror as a jeep followed a truck followed a couple of US Navy official cars, all propelled by many willing hands, along the quay and into the loch with a thunderous round of splashes. Then private cars, obviously picked from a list one of Bella's deputies was brandishing.

'Oh shit!' exclaimed Lewis Clarke. 'I guess the captain ain't going to be happy about this.'

'Sure as hell not, sir!' exclaimed Maitland Jnr. pointing to the far end of the car park where a crash of broken glass announced another side window smashed in to gain access. 'There goes the captain's three month old Mercedes! I would say someone is going to get their balls chewed off for losing that!'

Lewis Clarke cringed and felt sick. 'Mine.' he gasped quietly. 'As sure as shit it will be mine!'

For a moment he thought of rescinding his non interference order and telling the patrols to get ashore before the shiny Merc ended in the loch but just then the sound of many police sirens came from along the road as the local cops, no doubt called in by their patrol car that was permanently positioned up on the hillside above the base landing, tore along to try to put a stop to the vandalism. Too late for the captain's Merc though, for before the first cop car screeched to a halt by the gates, the Merc had been pushed off the shore end of the quay into the shallower water there, though it was still deep enough to submerge the new car in a flurry of protesting bubbles.

The assault stopped quickly after that, the sound of more sirens warning the Mothers that further reinforcements were on the way and their time was limited. Bella rallied her supporters and they beat a hasty retreat from the wrecked landing area and along the road to the relative safety of the unmapped Peace Camp which had all the complexity and ambush possibilities of a Moroccan souk. A previously chosen few lay down in the road in front of the approaching vehicles as a token sacrifice to the demands of the law, but Bella and her hard core of Mothers melted into the tumbled labyrinth of caravans, tents and huts to work out further strategy in their campaign against the might of the US Navy.

Lewis Clarke sat for a moment his eyes shut and pained, then returned to the quay, ordered the petty officer and his patrol ashore to retake the shambles there, then the other boat to take back the drenched marines and get them replaced. As the local police dragged the arrested protesters away for a brief holiday at the expense of Her Majesty's Government, he climbed up and surveyed the damage with growing dread then wearily climbed back down into the liberty boat.

'Back to the ship, Maitland.' he sighed. 'I'm gonna have to make a personal report to the captain, and I'm damned sure it's not going to be pleasant!'

The Peace Camp population varied at between sixty and three hundred bedraggled souls, depending on weather, weekends, willingness and the generosity of the local Social Security office, but the hard core was always there with its strident voluble leader in Bella Bolnay. The men of the camp were pale shadows alongside this Amazonian fanatic and as time passed she came to dominate them, bringing in more militant female recruits and borrowing even more militant ideas from other Peace Camps spread over Britain. She had recently returned from a recruiting drive on the battlefields of Greenham Common and had formulated her plans with cold calculation, her expected triumphant return only slightly marred by the near destruction of her mini-bus as it attempted to board the Fiddin Ferry. This was by no means forgotten, but she pushed it aside for the present, that ship would suffer later for that incident, and concentrated now on the greater goal.

She now gathered her fighting commando of followers around her, most of them excited and jubilant over their recent success.

'Shut up!' she yelled over this chattering din. 'You're like a bunch of twittering schoolgirls! We've achieved nothing with that attack except minor irritation so don't be misguided enough to start celebrating it.'

'We've got them on the run!' protested a tangled blonde.

'Rubbish!' Bella Retorted. 'They are still out in that loch with nuclear submarine alongside which has every missile still aboard and intact! And they'll stay that way out there until we have taken over that ship and proved how vulnerable they are. A few cars thrown in the loch does not even begin to threaten them!'

'Then what was all that about?' asked a rat haired brunette with a ring through her nose.

'I want their attention ashore.' Bella explained. 'I want them to concentrate most of the guard force on the jetty and I expect that will happen until the fence and the gate is properly repaired and reinforced. The more of those marines and SP's ashore the less there are on the ship, and that's our next target!'

The rat haired girl gave an exasperated sigh. 'We can't swim, and we don't have a good enough boat.'

'It's been tried.' a dusky ring tailed Rastafarian all the way from deepest darkest Deptford pointed out. 'Those patrol boats are not all that big, but baby, they are steel hulled and tough as walnut shells. They just rammed our boats and smashed them up. Then picked us off when we were half drowned and handed us over to the fuzz! There's not a lot of protesting you can do with a gob full of water!'

'Then we have to get a bigger and tougher boat than they have!' Bella gritted out with her teeth showing white and sharp.

'We'll need a floating tank then,' the Rastafarian pointed out. 'And an invisible one at that!'

Bella rounded on the chocolate coloured Londoner. 'The second part is where you come in. Take forty or so of the camp followers and start a protest outside the gate of the car park tonight. The cops won't touch you as long as you do not cross the road but make enough of a fuss there and they won't notice anything come in from the sea.'

'And the boat?' asked the tangled blonde.

'That's my part of the operation.' smiled Bella wickedly. 'I know the very craft and it will be a personal pleasure relieving the owner of it!'

The Dhu Mohr, though a sturdy enough craft in her time, could hardly be called a floating tank, for few tanks were infested by invisible but still destructive colonies of woodworm to the extent she was. Not enough to cause more than trivial leakage, but enough to make the average storm around the Clyde a danger to her ability to float.

Hector never took her out in anything but the best of weather these days. In this case though it mattered little, for Bella had no intention of using it or any other wooden fishing boat.

No doubt, if known, this would have been of some comfort to its two man crew who sat around with some amusement watching the debacle on the quay, and the grim expression of Commander Lewis Clarke as he made his way back to the base ship.

'Yon American fella did not half give us a dirty look as he went past.' Hector observed as he put down his big brass telescope which he had spent at least an hour polishing up. 'You would have thought it was us that threw him in the loch, instead of himself that done it.'

'No doubt he is not feeling friendly towards anyone right now.' Donald replied. 'Maybe he expected us to be giving him a wee hand, though I for one would not be wanting to tackle that wild bunch of witches again.'

Hector thought about it for a moment. 'No, nor I. Not after you telling me about their dirty fighting methods. It is not that often that I get a chance of a wee bit fun and games these days but I would like to keep my equipment intact in case the occasion arises.'

He took up his telescope again to look at a large patrol boat approaching from the base ship. 'It looks like they are going to land a fair big team at the jetty. There must be a couple of dozen of those marine fellows aboard that boat.'

Donald scanned the craft with his binoculars. 'There is that too.' He sat back to ponder for on this new arrangement. 'Now there is a thing, I would not be thinking that they would be letting any of their boys have shore leave this afternoon, even if they had the transport, and by the looks of that car park, there is not a lot of that left.'

'There is always Kerr's bus service, Donald, though I

doubt if the Yanks, with all their fancy computers and spy satellites, could work out what time the bus would be likely to turn up at the jetty.'

'Never the less, I know a few of them do use it.' Donald replied. 'Maybe being submarine men has taught them a lot of patience. But I would be thinking that the captain will not be letting his sailors the chance. No doubt those already ashore will find their way back, but I do not think any more will be let ashore after that ruckus a wee while back and the mob now moving down from their camp towards the car park.'

Hector focused his telescope on the shore again and saw some forty of the Mothers moving down in a chanting mob while the boat load of Marines armed with nightsticks hurried ashore and took up positions behind the damaged but still defendable fence. Between the two opposing side were now half a dozen police cars and some very hard and determined looking police who were well used to dealing harshly with the Mothers against Polaris, and well did the Mothers know this.

'Stalemate, would you think. Donald?'

'Very likely, Hector. Those harridans know the local police will not hold back.'

'Then we might as well be getting back to Greenock.' Hector said cheerfully. 'Unless you would be wanting to cut round to Fiddin on the way back for a couple of drams?'

The policeman gave a long regretful sigh. 'Much as I would like to Hector, I am afraid I cannot. I promised the wife I would take her to see that new film that is on at the Regal. Not that I am all that keen as I hear it is a right weepy, but a promise is a promise, and I fine know that if I went with you to Fiddin, I would end up spending the night there!'

'At least you would be among friends there.' Hector

pointed out. 'Not among all those foreigners like the Paddies and the Tallies that are hanging about over the river there!'

'Don't be so biased, Hector. Some of them are fine people and most of them have been around here for a couple of generations.'

'Well, your pet Sassenach has not! So, if you are wanting me to go up and speak to him tonight, I will be having a couple of drams in the town first!'

'I think that will not cause any great problems, Hector.' agreed Donald, feeling the need himself every time he had to go in and report to the customs man. As they had nothing really to report that day, as usual, Hector would be useful, embellishing the events of the day with his strong accent and Highland charm to the point the customs man quickly sent them away. It had worked a couple of times, and appealed to Hector's sense of humour, that is, take the Mickey out of the English at every opportunity. Now, I think we will be waiting for the next liberty boat that is scheduled, which is in about half an hour's time, and if there is nobody going ashore in that, then I doubt if anyone will be going ashore the rest of the day. So there will be no need to hang around and we will get ourselves back to Greenock and tell Smythe Smith nothing is happening.'

'I suppose that makes sense.' agreed Hector. 'Aye, it does that.' he continued, quite happy to agree to anything that got his big rough hands round a dram glass a bit earlier than usual.

The two cousins settled down to wait out the half hour, doing nothing much at all, for it was as pleasant a way of spending the afternoon as any other.

A few hundred yards away another man was not having a pleasant afternoon at all. The captain of the base ship glowered over his desk at Lewis Clarke and was slowly turning purple with rage as he read the hastily written report of the incident in the car park. It looked like an explosion was coming at any moment, and most likely in the direction of the unfortunate commander.

'What the hell is going on around here!?' the bull necked and bulging captain yelled. 'A bunch of crazy women are making a horse's ass out of the elite branch of the whole goddamn United States Navy!'

He threw the slightly damp report across the desk at Lewis Clarke. 'That Merc cost me fifteen thousand bucks! Now it's lying rotting at the bottom of this goddamn loch along with half the base shore transport!'

Lewis Clarke cringed and tried to slip in some good news. Sort off. 'Ah, sir, the salvage guys are rigging a barge now which should have your car out in a couple of hours and the ship's engineers say they can probably have it fixed by the next day.'

The captain gritted his teeth. 'And I suppose they can also sew new leather seats into it as well. Don't be so damn stupid, commander, it was brand new, now it's not! It's a piece of dunked garbage! Even Mercedes can't fix garbage to a brand new condition!'

'I did warn you sir.' the commander ventured tentatively. 'Those Mothers are a mean and nasty lot. We should have more guards ashore and a much stronger fence on the car park.'

'We are supposed to keep a low profile here, commander! Not turn the place into an armed fortress!'

Lewis Clarke wondered for a moment what difference that would make. Having at times enough nuclear firepower lying alongside to obliterate most of Britain and half Europe meant that this base represented much more than even the biggest fortress in history ever had. He shivered and carried on. 'We need more men ashore tonight sir, they are rigging a temporary fence and gate but it won't last two minutes if they make another attack like that.'

The captain glowered at him again but finally nodded. 'As many as you like then, but no arms. A few billy-clubs are okay but even then keep them out of sight. Now, have you any reason to believe they will attack again tonight?'

The commander muttered something, caught the captains warning glance, and decided it might be better to speak up. 'I don't know, sir.'

'The hell you don't, Clarke!' roared the captain. 'You are the man who is paid to know what these Mothers are up to! You are supposed to be watching them!'

'I'm sure it's something to do with that fishing boat!' Lewis Clarke protested in defence. 'Couldn't I just board it once sir? I'm sure I could find some evidence that they are communist agents and are in cahoots with that mob ashore.'

The Captain thumped his fist on the desk so hard the grey metal desk jumped and boomed like the drums of doom. 'You will not do that!' roared the captain. 'It doesn't matter if they are Communists or Methodists! That's a Brit boat out there, and as far as we can see it is legitimately fishing, and it is outside our patrol perimeter. You touch it without hard evidence and the Brit press will have a field day, and I will have your balls, mister!'

'Then there's nothing I can do, sir.' the commander muttered miserably.

'Like hell there's nothing!' The desk got thumped again and Clarke could have sworn the legs splayed out slightly and then sprung back in again. 'There's something rotten going on over at that damn slum camp over there and you'd better find out what it is!' The Captain leant over the much abused desk and glared at the commander. 'One more incident like today's fiasco, and I'll find you another job which will make your present position seem like a holiday. Like maybe at some far north radar station counting geese flying over Greenland!'

The Dhu Mohr was soon cutting across the River Clyde to her usual berth in Greenock, the two men having watched the liberty boat going ashore empty and only briefly stop at the quay to pick up a few returning sailors who had braved the blockade of the chanting Mothers.

'That looks like it.' Donald had said. 'The afternoon boat is usually packed with sailors heading into town, but there is not a soul today. We might as well be going.'

Hector had wasted no time in hauling up the anchor and setting out for a few highly anticipated whiskies across the river. Soon the cousins were propping up the bar in a rather dingy Greenock pub, discussing the events of the day and the possible reactions of the highly unpredictable customs superintendent.

'You would not be thinking that the man will be wanting me to hang about over here?' asked Hector between sips of an eight year old Highland malt.

'Hard to know what that man would want.' Donald replied. 'But just in case, you had better come up to the office with me.'

'Then I will be having another dram then, if you would not be minding, Donald.'

He waved his glass at the barman who appeared to be more interested in picking a horse to run in the two o'clock race at Doncaster. Being well after that hour it was hard to see where the interest lay, but then, as the paper he was diligently marking horses off in was two days old, the time hardly mattered. Eventually he dragged himself away from the paper and reluctantly served the two men.

Hector glanced around the rather seedy bar. A few of the wealthier patrons were drinking whisky, but most of the rest were on beer or the local favourite, a rather sweet and obnoxious cheap wine.

'I do not suppose we would bump into your Englishman in an establishment like this? I even heard from young Bell that the man does not even drink whisky.'

'Gin!' stated Donald with open disgust.

'Gin?' repeated Hector, in a similar manner, but as if he was asking what that was. 'Well maybe that was the strange perfumed smell I caught off him yesterday evening. Mind you, I thought I also caught the whiff of something more like sheep's manure!'

Donald downed the last of his whisky. 'Manure or not, we had better be heading up to see the man. I still have a wife to take to the cinema tonight.'

'I suppose so.' Hector said reluctantly. 'Though I am thinking that I would sooner be going up to talk to the sheep. I believe I would get more sense out of them.'

Smythe Smith was busy shuffling around some obscure written reports on practically nothing when the two cousins arrived at the office to make their report on that afternoon's incident. He listened quietly making the odd positive or negative grunt as the story unfolded, though at times he had to rack his brain to decipher Hector's contribution made with the usual elaboration and Highland accent.

'Quite right.' he finally said. 'No point in hanging around if nobody is going ashore. It's my opinion that that lot of bloody protestors are half crazy on dope anyhow. I'll warrant a raid on that camp would pull in a tidy haul.'

The sergeant paled at the idea of mixing it again with the formidable Mothers against Polaris and quickly tried to Scotch the idea. 'It's not really in our jurisdiction, is it, Superintendent? We would not be wanting to waste our time on a few petticoat junkies when there are bigger fish in the ocean to catch.'

Smythe Smith thought about it for a moment 'Quite right, Sergeant.' he said pompously. 'A waste of our valuable time, and not really in our terms of reference.'

What those terms were Smythe Smith had never been told and no amount of correspondence with HM Customs and Excise headquarters in London had ever even got a reply concerning this. He had though, in his own self centred way, always assumed that he had been sent to the wilds of Strathclyde to land the "big fish", and continued to act on that assumption.

'To get back to our proper business then, Sergeant.' he continued. 'I want to hear what happened on the Farnhead this morning.'

'Nothing much at all, sir, we delivered a few stores, had a wee bit of a chat with the crew, then picked up a couple of parcels to bring back.'

'What kind of parcels, and where are they now?' the customs officer demanded to know.

'Well there was a box of official papers to be mailed off to the shipping companies office and another parcel of football scarves which Angelo's cousin will be picking up in the morning. We dropped both of them off at the ship chandlers on the way here.'

'Then I'm heading there right now!' exclaimed Smythe Smith. 'I don't trust those damn Italians. Football scarves indeed! They must think we are entirely stupid!'

Hector raised his brows and gave a small smile. 'My, my, Superintendent, nobody would be thinking such a thing about you. Who but yourself would have thought that yon Indian hemp stuff could be knitted up into scarves? I myself would have thought it was too stringy and a bit on the smelly side to be hanging round your neck!'

Smythe Smith glared angrily at the whisky fortified

fisherman. Hector smiled nonchalantly back, and then got to his feet. 'Och well then,' he said. 'If I am not going to be wanted around here I might as well be heading back to Fiddin. I would not be wanting to run into that wee submarine in the dark.'

He turned and strolled towards the door but didn't quite get there.

'Hold it!' screeched Smythe Smith. 'What submarine? Where?'

Hector turned with a mock look of surprise. The sergeant slumped dejectedly into his chair. At times he wished Hector would give up his baiting of the superintendent and stop sending the man off on frantic wild goose chases.

Hector returned to the desk and leant over it. 'The little submarine that the Taffy twins on the Farnhead have been building themselves, of course.' he replied casually. 'The only one there is up Loch Fiddin. Even those Yankee sailors don't put their big black submarines up that loch, them being afraid of our monster!'

'A private submarine!' exclaimed Smythe Smith in anguish. 'And as usual I am the last person to hear about it! They've probably been smuggling tons of hashish and pounds of heroin in right under our noses!'

'Hardly likely.' assured Donald. 'The lads only put the boat into the water for the first time yesterday and tonight is the first time they will have been out for a dive in the dark.'

'With that submarine, maybe!' exclaimed the customs man. 'They could have a whole fleet of them operating up and down the coast for all we know!' He waved Hector to a chair, 'Sit down! I want to hear every detail of this submarine!'

Between the two cousins the details were fairly sparse as neither of them had taken a lot of notice of the actual design of the weird craft but Smythe Smith thought it was enough to confirm his suspicions. 'Treasure hunting in the loch? Utter sentimental rubbish and nobody wastes that much time looking for some supposed treasure that probably never existed.' He gave the others an outline of a plan of action and Donald cringed and gave Hector a glare when he realised he would have to call up his wife and cancel the cinema date. The plan would involve a lot of the evening, even going by the rough details Smythe Smith gave them, keeping the unformed details to himself.

'Right,' he finally said. 'I'm still going down now to check those parcels in the chandlers. Sergeant, Get a hold of Bell and Thomson and we will all meet down at the quay later.' He reluctantly turned to Hector. 'We'll need the use of your boat tonight.'

'I was just wondering when you would be getting around to asking.' Hector said with a small smile. 'Then of course, I will be asking for a bit more remuneration for risking my boat and my neck in Loch Fiddin in the dark. Say an extra two days charter money would I think be appropriate? There being monsters and smugglers and submarines all dancing a fine tune between the shores.'

Smythe Smith opened his mouth to protest this extortion, realised he had little choice about the matter, then shut it sharply and gave a reluctant nod.

'And I would like something in writing about it before we sail.' Hector added, turning the screw a little tighter. 'Not that I am an untrusting man, but should you be getting yourself eaten by the monster, I would be liking a little bit of paper to make my charter money claim with.'

Smythe Smith groaned at the thought of the massive amount of paper that would be involved in appropriating any extra money from his masters in London. 'All right!' he snapped. 'I'll have your bloody piece of paper for you when we meet at the boat!'

'That will be fine then,' Hector said graciously. 'And I will bring along some sandwiches as well. We can always be throwing them to the Loch Fiddin monster if it gets really hungry.'

Chapter 9

Round the corner from the monster besmitten loch, Angus Kerr sat in his tiny cabin aboard the Fiddin Ferry, last run of the day finished. Across in the even smaller galley, Gilly was preparing a basic meal for the three man crew, sustenance type food which really was all he could prepare, or all that the three men ever wanted. Tonight it was the old standby, mince and tatties, with the addition of a few carrots mixed in with the beef mince and even a bit of butter in the mashed potatoes. Life was good on the ferry, getting fed was a bonus.

Angus sat with a whisky in his hand but his customary companion for the end of day drink was missing, as he had been the previous night as well. The Chief Engineer of the sturdy craft had been sulking ever since his brusque dismissal from the bridge the previous day. McPhee had little time for the peace protestors but regarded his captain's actions against them as unprofessional, and the captain's brief display of anger towards him as unjustified and even more wrong.

McPhee was a strange one, thought Angus, a good friend for the last twenty years and a good engineer that had kept the ferry's engines ticking over all that time. The skipper poured himself another drink and gave a long contemplative sigh. Let the man eat his dinner himself tonight, tomorrow was another day.

A few hundred yards away it was that night's action that was clearly on the mind of the forty odd figures huddled round a motley collection of vehicles parked just out of sight of the ferry slipway at Garnock Point. Bella Bolnay and her Mothers against Polaris were planning vengeance against a recent antagonist combined with their continuing campaign against the American base. Bella was savouring the coming night like a tiger savouring a big fat tethered goat.

'Right girls,' she said after the brief huddled conference was over. 'You all have your orders. There are only three men on that piece of junk and two are too decrepit to put up much of a fight and the other appears to be a mindless idiot! Two minutes and we'll have them helpless and the ship will be ours!'

She stuck her clenched fist in the air in salute. 'Remember, if we succeed tonight, we will have struck a great blow for the peace movement in general and the Mothers against Polaris in particular!'

The commando clad and black faced figures faded into the darkness towards the slipway, some to release the ferry mooring ropes while a hard core made the initial assault on the ferry accommodation. Angus Kerr was on his third dram when he heard footsteps on the steel deck outside but thought little of it. Maybe, he thought briefly, McPhee had come out of his huff and decided to join him for dinner after all. Then he heard a muffled scream from the galley and the sound of breaking dishes.

'Damn it!' he exclaimed, more to himself than anyone else. 'That silly beggar Gilly has dropped my dinner!'

He stuck his head out of the cabin door and nearly had it pulled off as half a dozen big burly women grabbed him and dragged him struggling out the short alleyway and onto the car deck. Gilly was there already, four hefty women piled up on top of his slight body, and McPhee could be discerned beneath a similar pile of feminine ballast.

'Bloody bunch of pirates!' roared the skipper as he too was forced onto the deck, a particularly heavy specimen landing on his chest and knocking the wind out of him then a few more of the Mothers piled on top for good measure.

The ferry had been taken well within the predicted two minutes and another minute saw the three men securely trussed up with rope, like one rather plump turkey and a couple of scrawny chickens. Bella grinned wickedly and addressed the secured men. 'Your boat is now part of the campaign against nuclear weapons on the sacred soil of your country! Tonight we strike a blow for freedom when we invade the American imperialist naval base.'

Angus Kerr, fighting to get his breath, was not intimidated at all. 'Away you daft fat Sassenach, my country and yours have damn little in common, but this is my ship and it will have no bloody part in anything unless I want it to! I'll string you bunch of piddling pirates up from my bridge when I get my hands on you!'

'You capitalist chauvinist pigs are all the same!' shouted Bella into his face. 'Always making threats you are in no position to carry out!'

She turned to her jubilant troops. 'Cart the fat man up to his steering position. We'll show him who is running this boat.'

Several of the women started to drag the corpulent captain up the narrow stairs to the bridge but soon found the task impossible. The sheer bulk of the skipper blocked the stairway, as it nearly did in normal circumstances. After a brief unequal struggle with gravity and narrow dimensional limits, and receiving no cooperation at all from their captive, the exhausted women had to admit defeat.

Bella swore like a taxi driver and had to change her carefully laid plans. The turned and looked around and saw the skinny figure of Gilly almost buried under a couple of women. 'You'll steer!' she informed him brusquely.

'I damn well won't!' said the suddenly determined seaman come general hand.

Bella glared at him then smiled wickedly 'Strip him!' she commanded her followers.

Gilly found himself sat on again but this time carefully and with wicked intent, many enthusiastic hands ripping of his clothes. Shoes, socks, trousers and shirt were torn from his trembling body and strewn about the deck and when they got to his underclothes he caved in.

'I'll steer!' he screamed. 'I'll steer the bloody ferry!'

'It's nice to have a willing volunteer.' Bella said caustically. 'Untie him and take him up top, If he tries anything---.'

She left the rest unsaid but Gilly had no doubts what would happen if he made any unwise moves.

Once untied, he gathered the remains of his clothing and tied it roughly round him, trying to ignore the pointed comments from the women and the nasty look from his captain.

'Traitor!' shouted Angus Kerr as Gilly stepped onto the bridge ladder. 'I will remember this later.'

'I'll not forget it myself.' Gilly shouted back. 'I'm only here to do a job and if you hadn't annoyed these bliddy women we might not be in this position! I'll be seeing my union about this!'

'Stuff your union, you feart wee man!' Angus added, for unions he liked about as much as his present assailants. 'See if waving your damn union card at this lot will be doing you any good at all!'

Bella turned and scowled at the captain. 'Gag this one! He's got far too much to say for himself and we don't need the organ grinder when we have the monkey.'

The captain, shouting and cursing was duly gagged though these soon turned to mumbles.

She turned to McPhee and gave him a warning look, but the engineer had recovered from his surprise and initial rough handling but was still peeved at his treatment from the captain the day before. He just shrugged as he looked up at the bloody determination on Bella's face.

'There's no need for any carry on.' he said quietly, but not so quietly that the skipper could not hear him, causing Angus Kerr to go even redder in the face. 'I'm only the poor bloody engineer of this boat! You ring that telegraph up there and I'll work the engines.'

'Turn him loose.' instructed Bella. 'But two of you stay with him to make sure he doesn't change his mind!'

McPhee was untied then addressed the protesters in general. 'I told that old fool of a skipper no good would come of that carry on yesterday.' He turned then to his skipper. 'Sure as blazes you are going to lose your pissing council subsidy after this carry on!'

Angus puffed up fit to burst his gag and glared wildly at the engineer who promptly turned on his heels and headed for the engine room door, escorted by two of Bella's favoured storm troopers. 'I'm not getting stripped off in front of a bunch of crazy women for the sake of any boat.' He muttered. 'I do have my dignity, you know!' He disappeared down the stairs, head held high, and dignity intact.

Bella pushed her way up into the tiny wheelhouse and two of her Lieutenants crammed in beside her and the still quaking Gilly. The mooring ropes already gone, only the slight friction of the ramp held the ferry in place, so she asked Gilly to lift it.

'I'm sorry missus.' he said fearfully. 'But I canna do that.'

Bella glared at him and repeated her demand and Gilly turned paler under her ferocious gaze.

'I'm never normally up her, missus when we leave or

berth.' he protested. 'I can steer but I don't really know anything about running the boat except collecting tickets!'

Bella stared in horror at the seaman, then in equal horror at the mixture of levers and buttons on the control consul. They baffled her as much as they did the seaman, and in truth they would have even baffled the builders of the ferry thirty years before. Over the years McPhee's ingenuity had been hard at work, adapting and modifying, but seldom labelling. He knew, his skipper knew, so why clutter the console up with unnecessary labels?

'Can the boat sail with the ramp down?' Bella enquired hopefully.

'No bother at all, missus.' Gilly replied brightly. It's only a safety precaution to stop the cars and the passengers falling off.'

Bella stuck her head out the wheelhouse and bawled to her followers. 'Get away from the ramp and hold onto something solid!'

She turned back to Gilly. 'Well, what are you waiting for? Get the damn boat moving!'

'You'll have to ring that telegraph for the engine then.' said Gilly cautiously, pointing the large brass instrument next to Bella.

Bella angrily pulled the lever down. Nothing happened for a moment then a whistling came from the old voice pipe next to the telegraph. After a bit of fiddling around Bella shouted something unintelligible down the pipe just like she had seen one time in an old movie.

McPhee's sarcastic tones answered back. 'I take it you are not intending to go overland to the Yankee ship? That being so, would you put the telegraph to the ahead position, then maybe we could get going.'

Bella swore but checked the lettering on the shiny instrument. Years of severe polishing had taken its toll and though the brass had survived in gleaming condition, the

embossed lettering on the face had almost disappeared. – ull–ead had survived in faint letters, more like the name of some obscure Scottish cape than an instruction to put
the engine to Full Ahead. Eventually, using a torch that sat nearby, she deciphered the obscured letters. It was marked through from Full Ahead to Full Astern with variations and a Stop position in between. She looked at Gilly who shook his head. 'Nae use in asking me, missus, I can steer and I can blow the hooter, but that's about it!'

Bella swore again, suspecting that the seaman knew more than he was letting on, but cautiously put the telegraph to the Slow Ahead position with a small clang, heard an answering clang from the engine room, and the engine coughed into life. The ferry shuddered a little as the propeller bit but didn't move, held by the ramp on the rough concrete of the slipway. She shoved the telegraph to Full Ahead and the engines roared in protest before the ship lurched then it scraped off the concrete with a tortured screech and out into the dark waters of the river.

'How the blazes do you know which end is which!' Bella shouted after realising that the boat could be steered and controlled in both directions.

'That's easy, missus.' Gilly replied. 'Just keep in mind that the stern ramp is down, and the bow ramp is up.'

'And what if both ramps were up?'

'Ah, but they are not tonight. Any other time the skipper would be up here and I am sure that after running the boat for thirty years he can probably tell the difference.'

Gilly seemed quite pleased with this observation and though Bella wanted to rip his throat out she gritted her teeth and gave up in disgust. She had met a few of these stoic Scots philosophers before, otherwise known as the village idiots, and knew it was a waste of time to argue against their brand of logic. At least he was watching what he was doing, spinning the wheel round like he knew what he was doing, so she didn't really worry too much.

She should have, for Gilly was having a great number of problems. True, he could steer, but had never steered this ferry before, especially backwards, and add that to the peculiarities of its double ended shape and he had not the faintest idea what direction he was heading in.

'Ehhhh, mmm-missus.' he stammered frantically. 'Which way do you want me to go?

'I thought you said you could steer?' asked Bella sharply.

'I do know how to steer!' Gilly retorted in an offended voice. 'But somebody has to tell me where to steer!'

'Steer to the American base ship!' she demanded.

'And what direction is that supposed to be in?' Gilly asked. 'You tell me that and I'll be quite happy to steer you there, for I am not too happy about wandering about in the dark especially with the Garnock Rocks none too far away.'

By this time the ferry had careened its way out into the wide reaches of the river on a rather erratic and totally unknown course. The realisation that there could be a set of razor sharp rocks waiting out there hit all three women and the only man on the bridge at the same time. Around them lay miles of dark estuarial water, unlit by the cloud hidden moon, and ringed by necklaces of shore bound lights of varying intensity. At all points of the compass other lights winked on and off, but there was no flashing neon sign pointing to the American base.

Bella's companions began to squeak slightly and she recognised the signs of impending panic. Like all good generals she swung into the attack, rounding on the unfortunate seaman beside her as the best target.

'Put the bloody headlights on, you fool, and then maybe we can see where we are going!'

'Don't be calling me a fool!' Gilly snapped back, his

fear turning to anger at these crazy women who were risking his neck. 'It's you daft women who are fools! Ships don't have headlights!'

Bella was furious, as well as slightly frightened at the situation, which appeared to be rapidly getting out of her control. 'Then how the hell do you manage to see in the dark?'

'Navigation lights, you big daft Sassenach!' the suddenly brave Gilly shouted back just as loud.

'Don't you swear at me you horrible little haggis eater!' she yelled. 'One more smart remark out of you and I'll have the girls do the business on you properly this time!'

'I'm not frightened to of any bunch of lassies.' Gilly sneered, the previous encounter forgotten. 'You lot try anything and I'll have my union on you! I'll strike, and then see how you get on!'

Bella was forced to see the logic of this argument. This little porridge eater was not much good but he did know a little, and she had no wish to spend the night wandering about in the waters of the Clyde looking for some rocks to sit on. But just wait till later, she thought, and then this tartan twerp would really suffer!

'Switch on the navigation lights then.' She paused and nearly chocked saying it. 'Please!'

Triumphant in this small victory, Gilly smiled wickedly at her. 'They are on.' he said with a shrug.

'Then why can't we see?' she moaned.

'We are not meant to see them! It's other ships that are meant to see ours and we are meant to see there's.' He pointed out to the bridge wings. 'They're on the outside of the ship and only those little green and red indicator lights show to let me know they are on.'

Gilly was highly pleased at this piece of superior knowledge. He had accidentally put them on when he had been putting on other lights on deck and in the wheelhouse, but he wasn't going to admit that he didn't know which were which. Well not yet anyway.

Bella was almost loosing it completely now. She wished she had never started this carry on without some sort of expert in nightime navigation but gritted her teeth and shook herself, determined to carry on.

'Then the Yanks would see the boat coming?' she asked anxiously.

'Sure thing, missus. You can see our navigation lights for miles.'

'Put them off!' she demanded.

Gilly looked aghast at the woman. 'You canna put off a ships navigation lights at night! It's against the law!'

'Put them off!' snarled Bella, her teeth bared and her fury causing he face to twist into a demon shape.

Gilly realised he was stepping a bit close to actual physical damage and tried ignorance again. 'Ah don't know where the switches are!'

But his eyes betrayed him as he involuntarily glanced towards the small switchboard at the back of the wheelhouse. Bella pounced, flicking off switch after switch. The ferry plunged into darkness and the little indicator lights finally flickered off. Screams echoed up from the inky darkness of the car deck where the rest of her commandos were gathered and she rushed out to the bridge wing to reassure her troops.

'It's all right girls!' she yelled. 'It's all part of the plan. Just hang onto the sides!'

A few plaintive voices called back and Bella gave a few more assurances before returning to the wheelhouse to confront Gilly.

'Where are we now? She demanded to know.

'I told you before, missus, I don't bliddy well know where we are! You'll have to get the skipper up!'

'Never!' she screamed causing Gilly to jump back and

even her own supporters to jerk and shake. 'The man's a fascist! I'd sooner sink!'

'I'd sooner not, missus! I canna swim!'

'Then find the bloody base!' Bella's voice had a very hard edge now, fear, anger and inability to control the situation turning into a dangerous mix. 'If you can't find it there is no point in you being around and you might have to learn to swim very quickly!'

Gilly gritted his teeth and looked around desperately. By luck the ferry had virtually crossed the river and was closing in on an unmistakable swath of lights. 'That's Greenock!' he exclaimed with an audible sigh of relief. 'We're going the wrong way, so I suppose we'd better be turning around.'

'Then turn!' snarled Bella with a savageness that even frightened her two supporters on the bridge. She believed she had this little heather hugger frightened again and meant to keep him that way.

Gilly hastily turned the wheel hard over. The little ferry gave a violent shudder and began to swing, its old hull creaking and groaning in protest as it heeled over at an appalling angle that it had never been subjected to in all its working life. More screams arose from the deck as the Mothers down there were thrown across the car deck adding to the heel and causing water to slop along the edge of the deck.

Even Bella went horribly cold as she hung on grimly to the control console but Gilly got the wheel back quickly and the hull straightened up with a loud smack on the flat bottom. Bella gulped then rushed out to assure her supporters, as the two already on the bridge huddled together in moaning fear.

Then the engine room door opened flooding light out on the deck over a tangled group of women, and a very angry McPhee stamped out his face a mask of fury. He glanced disdainfully at the group at his feet, then roared up at the bridge.

'Are you lot bliddy insane? You any idea what you are doing? You damn near turned the boat over! It was never built to do that kind of manoeuvring at full speed!'

'Then slow it down!' Bella roared back.

'Then bliddy well ring the telegraph!' McPhee snarled. 'How the hell am I supposed to know what you idiots are up to?'

He stepped back inside and slammed the engine room door shut behind him, again plunging the deck into darkness.

Bella jumped back into the wheelhouse and pushed the brass telegraph pointer back to its central position. The ferry slowly drifted to a halt, its bows, or stern, or whatever it was, pointing across the dark waters of the firth.

'Right!' she snapped with anger fed determination. 'We stay here till we find out exactly where to go. I'm going to see that bloody fascist of a captain, and by the time I'm finished with him he'll be begging to come back up here!'

She turned to the two snivelling supporters. 'Keep an eye on this one. He takes his hands off that wheel, do what you bloody well like with him.'

Gilly stared at her, then at the snivelling girls, and shook his head. He should be worried about them?

Bella glowered at Gilly, realised the position she was in, and then pounded off down the ladder to Angus Kerr's cabin.

Sitting in his cabin across the firth Commander Lewis Clarke was totally unaware of the impending invasion of his territory. At that moment he was thinking of writing out his tenth request of the month for a transfer back to the good old U.S.A. Even Alaska would be preferable to this nutty country! At least there, all you had to worry about were the usual bunch of crazy American environmentalists and religious freaks, not mad Scotsmen blasting out at you with shotguns and even madder women attacking the base.

The events of the previous two days weighed heavily on his mind, the only glimmer of hope being the report of the recently returned Padowski about the strange silent craft on Loch Fiddin. There was something weird going on over there, and the first chance he got he was going back to investigate. A successful mission was his only chance of redeeming himself in the eyes of that old ball breaker of a captain and he had to take every chance he could get.

He poured himself another glass of totally unofficial whisky. It was the only thing with a damn in this god-forsaken country though truthfully he felt a little guilty about it, a good old American bourbon would have been more patriotic. He upended the bottle, the last few drops of the amber liquid fell reluctantly into his glass. He seemed to recollect the bottle was half full when he finished ploughing his way through the usual mountain of bullshit paperwork and settled down for only a couple of drinks. Ah well, what if he had a couple more?

Damn it, a man is entitled to a drink after a hard day's work, even if the United States Navy did not approve.

He downed the fiery liquor in a swift gulp and headed down to the mess for a quick supper before turning in for the night. Stuff the commies, and stuff the Mothers against Polaris! Now there was a thought. Stuff them all with dynamite and blow them all to hell!

He lurched slightly as he moved along the steel alleyway of the base ship, his empty since lunchtime stomach boiling slightly on the more than liberal dose of drink. The lights seemed to flicker and the walls seemed to move erratically. He stopped and pulled himself upright. No damn Scot's booze was going to get the better of a red blooded American boy!

'Evening, Commander.'

A foggy but familiar face confronted him. Clarke managed to focus on the man. 'Ah, Padowski. You ain't out with your girl tonight?'

Padowski blushed furiously and lied. 'No sir, she's a bit tired out after walking about the hills today.'

Hot Helen was really more angry than tired, and had stamped away in fury to catch the ferry home after her humiliating experience on the hillside. Things did not look good for Padowski's future happiness.

The commander, unaware of this, continued with a leer. 'Sure thing, Padowski. Don' tire your little lady out to much. We might need her help again.'

Padowski doubted if that would ever happen now but ignored the remark, and as the commander tried to squeeze past, he held him by the shoulder partly to hold him up but also to detain him. 'I know I ain't paid to think, sir.' he said apologetically. 'But I think there's something you should know, sir.'

'What gives, Padowski?' the commander asked suspiciously.

'Well sir, I've just been talking to one of the guys from a patrol boat and he tells me they passed that fishing boat about ten minutes ago and it was heading for Loch Fiddin.'

Clarke staggered a bit then shook his head. 'No problem, Padowski. It heads back that way every night. Maitland already called and informed me.'

'Yes sir, I know that, I asked him about it.'

'So it's normal, Padowski, or as normal as anything is about this screwball country.'

The seaman, though his best instincts told him to remain silent, also knew that if his knowledge of events ever came out it would cause him a great deal of grief, took a deep breath and plunged right in. 'Sir, Maitland tells me from here you don't get a real good view of the fishing boat, but the guy from the patrol boat tells me they passed close by and instead of the usual single old timer aboard, there was a whole pile of people on it!'

Clarke staggered back into a fire hydrant that stuck out of the bulkhead for the sole purpose of causing hip bruises, and the nudge of pain almost caused him to sober up. 'Goddamn it! I should have known it! Whatever they lost up there must have been helluva important so now they've brought back a whole army to look for it!'

Padowski doubted very much that the numbers that could be accommodated on a small fishing boat could be considered "a whole army", but wasn't going to argue with a full blown commander, especially one who was clearly a little, or maybe a lot, intoxicated. He gulped and shut up, knowing the damage was done.

Lewis Clarke grabbed the seaman urgently. 'Get a hold of Maitland. Both of you put on some dark clothes and meet me down at the landing platform and arrange a boat to pursue those damn commies! Now move it, sailor!'

He propelled the seaman on his way and after another painful argument with the fire hydrant, lurched back along the alleyway to his own cabin. His old pappy's World War Two army revolver would be going out tonight, and the hell with regulations! If people shot at an officer of the United States Navy, the United States Navy had a duty to fire back! He quickly pulled on a dark jacket and watch cap, checked the illegal weapon, then stuck it inside the jacket and headed for the small boat landing sited near the stern of the ship.

A few minutes later all three of the party stood on the floating dock by the ships side. A bored looking marine stood there under a light guarding the landing, gum getting violently masticated in his mouth, and a rifle casually slung over his shoulder. Maitland, the first to arrive, had already questioned him about the availability of patrol and liberty boats having seen none sitting there. The answer he knew would not please the commander.

'What the hell do you mean there are no boats available?' Lewis Clarke growled when Maitland Jnr. made his report.

'Well sir, three boats just left on patrol and won't return for thirty minutes, another took two Brit officers who were visiting back to Greenock, one is in dock for repairs and the last boat to return from picking up guys from shore leave had its alternator burnt out after one guy threw up on the engine and nearly electrocuted himself.'

The commander went nearly purple with fury. 'Are you telling me the United States navy is in jeopardy because some idiot couldn't hold his liquor?'

'Looks like it sir.' Maitland replied with a shrug. 'We could use one of the work boats but it would take till morning to get round to Loch Fiddin in those waddling hulks. Or we could call in one of the patrol boats but that would take some time.'

The marine gave a faint guffaw attracting Lewis Clarke's attention. 'What do you find so funny?' the commander demanded to know.

The marine continued his chewing for a moment before answering, he could well afford to as his commander had nothing but contempt for this commander in front of him, and would back him to the hilt, never the less, he did answer. 'Chief PO Sitting Bull is personally in charge of the boat patrols tonight, Commander, and he is not the world's most approachable man.'

Lewis Clarke shuddered. That Chief PO was the captain's personal Rottweiler, a giant full blooded Native American who did not mind his nickname at all, and who was virtually the head honcho of the ship. The chances of getting a patrol boat from him were negative of zero.

'Maybe the captain would let you borrow his new toy.' continued the marine with more than a touch of sarcasm, gesturing towards the gleaming two deck Chris Craft that had been delivered only a few days before.

Lewis Clarke glanced round at the launch, which officially was included in the base assets simply for form, and shuddered at this reminder of his captain's power. Then he looked again. The lights on the landing stage shone on the craft and an answering twinkle shone back from the door of the control cabin. The keys were in the lock!

He leapt into the boat and quickly unlocked the door. The shiny new controls twinkled tantalisingly back at him like a hypnotist's swinging watch.

'Hey!' the marine shouted, suddenly alert to an appalling risk. 'The Old Man will have your balls if you even as much as scratch his new boat!'

'Stuff the Old Man!' Lewis Clarke shouted back determinedly. 'This is US Navy property, not his personally! And he'll give me a medal if I catch these commie bastards that are causing all the trouble around here!'

He gestured to Maitland Jnr. and Padowski. 'Cast the ropes off! We're heading out in style tonight!'

'Is that an order, sir?' asked the astounded duo almost simultaneously.

'It's a goddamn order all right!' Lewis Clarke screamed back. 'Now shake your goddamn butts!'

The pair looked at the marine who shook his head and moved back towards the small hut where there was an internal phone line, but otherwise was not wanting to be involved.

'Move it!' they were again told. 'The safety of the United States is at risk!'

Years of patriotic brain washing and relentless training kicked in and the men quickly, if reluctantly, obeyed the order then climbed gingerly into the powerboat as it drifted away with a push of a boathook. Lewis Clarke shouted across at the horrified marine. 'Now call that damn patrol boat back and tell them to follow us up Loch Fiddin!'

He turned and twisted the ignition key and the two powerful petrol outboards purred into life and the commander's smile near cut his face in two.

'I'll sure as hell tell them!' yelled back the marine. 'And when the captain hears you've taken his new boat the whole goddamn U.S. Navy this side of the Atlantic is likely to be following you up Loch Fiddin!'

Chapter 10

On the bridge of the Fiddin Ferry one of Bella's girls turned to Gilly, who sat quietly and tunelessly whistling in the corner. 'What are those coloured lights?' she enquired anxiously. 'They're coming closer.'

Gilly got up and strolled casually to the front of the wheelhouse and looked out, then stood there frozen for a few moments, face turning ashen with sheer horror. Small gurgling sounds came from his throat which quivered nervously till sound finally overcame fear and gushed out. 'Oh mother!' he screamed, then sprang into action. He slammed the telegraph hard forward and yelled frantically down the voice pipe. 'Chief! Chief! For God's sake! There's a bloody big boat near on top of us!'

The engines roared into life and the little ferry began to shudder and strain as it tried desperately to overcome its inertia and escape its likely fate.

A few moments before Gilly had sat gloating over the fate of his captain, whose stubbornness had been the cause of all this bother. A lot of bangs and screams had indicated that the skipper was putting up a fair struggle against Bella and his troops, and Gilly was happily anticipating the sight of a stark naked captain being paraded about his own ship! Oh what a tale that would make to tell in all the local pubs, and how many free drinks would that gain the seaman?

Now he had his doubts if he would ever see the inside of a local pub again, and was fervently wishing that his captain was now standing next to him on the bridge and in charge of the terrifying situation.

Slowly, but surely, the ferry began to move, and the praying seaman began to swing the sluggish steering wheel over. The twin red and green navigation lights were getting closer now and the white masthead lights of the approaching Armageddon seemed to loom over them and still heading straight for the little ferry.

'My God! My God!' gasped Gilly. 'They can't see us! That stupid bitch put our navigation lights out!'

The stupid bitch in question, the captains chastisement forgotten with the first frantic shudder of the engines, charged up the bridge stairs, scarf and shawl flying.

'What the hell is going on?' she demanded to know.

Gilly mumbled incoherently and pointed into the night. The massive silvery wet bows of a giant tanker, outward bound from the Finnart oil terminal, loomed over the little ferry, the bone between its teeth sending spray and waves across the water in a massive gaping threat that seemed miles wide. The rhythmic beat of its powerful engines now sounded over the water like the heartbeat of a huge dinosaur charging down on its prey, which was close to being crunched under that massive bulbous lip.

Bella and her girls hung on to the bridge rail, terror in their hearts and knuckles whitening in the cold night air.

'Faster!' screamed Gilly down the engine room voice pipe. 'Faster, or we're all dead!'

'The damn engines are near off their bedplates!' McPhee roared back. 'We can't go any faster!'

The ferry stern frothed and pounded, then slowly began to lift on the tanker's massive bow wave. Then it started to skid forward away from the cold hard steel wall as the ocean monster slipped astern of it. Foam boiled over the after ramp of the ferry and poured knee deep along the deck washing over a screaming mass of Mothers that would have been swept over the front if the corrugated flap of the bow ramp had not brought them up sharply in a sodden huddled mass. Then the tanker's secondary waves spun the ferry round, tilting it back and swirling the water out the stern, soaked howling women clinging desperately to every handhold and obstruction.

For a few minutes this seesaw movement continued as wave after wave tumbled the ferry around then at last the steel giant was past, the thrashing and highly visible propeller boiling the water behind it and throwing great splashes of water into its iridescent wake.

'Oh Mother!' cried the ashen faced Gilly one more time, then he quietly slipped down from the steering wheel in a dead faint.

McPhee, trapped down below and unable to get any sense from the bridge, slowed his precious engines and waited for the next crisis. Luckily the next voice he heard from the pipe was the captains, who had only taken a minute after that to be convinced that he would resume command of his ship.

'It was just not funny sitting there waiting on you bunch of idiots destroying my ship!' he told Bella after he had been freed and escorted to the bridge. 'Especially as it was happening every couple of minutes!'

He scanned round the firth, saw no more impending disasters, called up McPhee to hear if the engines were okay, then let them idle for a few moments till the mess down on the deck was sorted out. Incredibly none of the Mothers were missing, more the pity, he thought, nor even seriously injured, though there would be plenty of bruises to go round the next morning.

Bella was still suspicious of accepting help from this old fascist reprobate, but had to admit it had been frightening enough during those violent manoeuvres, without being stuck in a little cabin, bound and gagged. Besides, she had little choice as Gilly had proved a near waste of space and was huddled in the corner now muttering and crying and unlikely to be much good for some time.

Angus noted the lack of navigation lights as the ferry drifted around on the tide, but had shrugged acceptance when informed of the reason. He knew the traffic at night was next to nothing, and he could see their lights if they were around. In command again, he had his own plans, and these did not include wasting time arguing with a bunch of fanatical women.

'McPhee!' he called down the voice pipe. 'If it is all right with you, we will be taking these women across to the American base now.'

'I would not be thinking we have much choice, Captain.' McPhee sniffed. 'That is if the old boat hangs together long enough, for she has taken an awful hammering this last half hour or so.'

'She will be just fine, McPhee, just fine. Now just be giving your wee engines a tweak and we will be going.'

The captain brought the telegraph up to half ahead as the engines revved up a little and as it got under way, he increased to full ahead, heading across the river, casually steering with one hand. Bella waved a beefy threatening finger at him. 'No tricks! Or else!'

'No tricks, woman.' promised the nonchalant skipper, hastily crossing his fingers behind the wheel. 'I give you my word on my deep sea masters certificate.'

Bella felt reassured by this solemn vow, but she was not to know that Angus had never held such a treasured document, having only reached the rank of mate deep sea before settling down to life on the ferries. He had no intention of keeping his word anyhow, as he was only there under threat.

Angus gestured towards the now conscious but still badly shaken Gilly who sat huddled in the corner of the bridge. 'I think you had better get one of your lassies to take him below and give him a couple of whiskies. The boy has had a fair fright and is in need of a peg or two. There was a bottle sitting in the desk of my cabin, though I dare say it's more likely to be rolling about the floor now.'

'No!' exclaimed Bella. 'I want him up here where I can keep an eye on him! We'll bring the whisky up.'

'Yes!' snapped Angus, who wanted Gilly well away from the vantage point of the bridge. 'The boy is needing a half, but I will not be having strong drink on my bridge!'

To emphasize his point he swung the telegraph back to Stop and stood there defiant as the ferry again shuddered to a halt.

'You've been drinking yourself, you old hypocrite!' yelled Bella, pushing Angus aside and slamming the telegraph to Full Ahead.

'I was drinking in my cabin!' the skipper roared back. 'Whether I am drunk, sober or crazy down there matters not a tinker's damn! But nobody will drink on the bridge as long as I am skipper of this vessel!'

He promptly used his slightly superior weight to push Bella aside and then slammed the telegraph back to Stop.

Bella's countermove was stopped by the determined skipper and a brief struggle ensued during which the telegraph was briskly rattled back and forth. The engines rumbled to a stop and a shrill whistle came from the voice pipe distracting both parties before McPhee's voice caustically echoed out of it.

'Are you all having a wee bit if fun up there, or am I supposed to answer all these movements?' he asked.

It was Bella that was first to shout back. 'This drunken old fool won't let anyone drink on his precious bridge. He thinks he's the captain of the QE2 or something!'

There was a studied silence from the engine room then McPhee answered in strong, steady tones. 'I have my own personal dispute with Captain Angus Kerr, madam, but, while he, or any other captain for that matter, is in command of a ship, not even an Admiral of the Fleet would be allowed as much as a glass of herbal wine on the bridge! Now, if you want my cooperation, and I can assure you madam that you are going nowhere without it, then you had better do what my Captain wants!'

Bella looked around. Angus was pointedly standing with his back to the wheel, arms firmly folded. Gilly sat slumped and uncaring in the corner, as much use as a squashed hedgehog, and Bella's girls, pale faced and frightened, looked at her appealingly.

She gritted her teeth. 'All right then!' she spat furiously gesturing to her girls. 'Get some of the others and get this weakling below and pour some Dutch courage into him! We might need him again.'

She reluctantly turned back to Angus after a couple of the soaked women from the deck hurriedly half carried Gilly down and out of sight. 'Now, can we get going again?'

Angus nodded his assent as she waved a warning digit at him. 'I want to know every move you make and why you are making it. Clear!'

Angus shrugged agreement and leaned over the voice pipe. 'My thanks, Mister McPhee, I could not have put the situation more eloquently myself. Now, can you start the engines, please? Oh, and chief, you had maybe be looking after your sea suctions, there is likely to be a bit of weed about the loch entrance, especially on the east side.'

'Weed?' queried McPhee quietly. 'There is no---.' The engineer stopped then raised his voice. 'Och aye, skipper. With the state of the tide, I imagine, there will be a fair bit of weed at the entrance to some of the lochs. I will be very careful about it.'

A few moments later the engines again roared into life and the ferry again started making its way across the river.

'How do you know where you are going?' Bella asked.

'Where are your charts?'

Angus gave her a look almost of contempt but the small twist to his mouth was lost in the near dark. He tapped the side of his head. 'Thirty years on this river so I know where all the lights are and what they mean.' He pointed out a bright clutter in the gloom. 'Over there, that cluster of lights is round the base ship. It is a little bit misty but still easy to pick out. We just head for them and we will be all right.'

'There's nothing in between?' Bella asked, a bit suspicious still.

'Only a couple of wee rocks which I would know in my sleep, and deep enough that my shallow draft ship would run over them anyhow. You do not for a moment think I would be daft enough to run my fine wee ship up on one of them, do you? Just be patient woman, and we will be there in no time.'

Angus gave a small and unintended chuckle that caused Bella to quickly turn on him, eyes glaring suspiciously.

The captain coughed slightly. 'A bit of a bite in the air tonight.' he said gruffly clearing his throat. 'It fair catches in an old man's throat.'

'Why are we turning away from the lights of the ship?' Smythe Smith asked as the Dhu Mohr chugged into the entrance to Loch Fiddin.

'The direct route up the east side of Fiddin Island is pretty shallow.' explained the sergeant. 'We will be cutting round the west side up the deep water channel then it is a direct run up to the Farnhead.'

The Customs man nodded as if he knew that already. 'Very good, sergeant, and a smugglers boat could not go round that way?'

The sergeant shrugged. 'A wee boat like this could get through at high tide, which is about now, in fact, but anything bigger would probably run aground. Only sand and mud, mind you, but there is a lot of weed in the channel and you have to be careful where you go.'

'Desperate men would take that chance though!' Smythe Smith exclaimed.

Hector snapped round from his position at the wheel and glowered at Smythe Smith, the slight up-light from the compass making his normally benign looking face look weird and fierce. 'Maybe they would,' he growled. 'But I am just a simple fisherman, not a desperate man, and I will not be taking a chance like that!'

Smythe Smith backed away quickly. 'No no, I hope it will not be necessary!'

He turned and spoke to the two other customs men who sat on the raised skylight behind the little wheelhouse. 'Keep a good lookout.' he huffed. 'If there are any smugglers in the area they may try to sneak across the shallows on the other side of the island.'

Tinkle Bell turned in mock amazement to Jimmy Thomson and shook his head in wonder before turning back to his superior.

'Tell me, super, why would they want to go across the shallows in a submarine?'

Smythe Smith glowered at them but couldn't find an answer. 'Just watch the damn loch and keep quiet!' he hissed angrily.

The darkened Fiddin ferry was only half a mile behind the Dhu Mohr as it entered the loch. Slowed down for the approach all on board could see the lights of a large ship through the thin mist but the fishing boats lights were obscured by the high trees of the little island.

Angus Kerr whistled down the voice tube. 'McPhee, we will maybe be getting a little weed in a couple of minutes.'

'Aye, sure thing, Angus.' came the reply, the tone of

voice reassuring the skipper and the use of his Christian name letting him know all was forgiven. 'I know just fine where we are and what to expect.'

'What's this business about weed?' the ever wary Bella asked abruptly. 'The loch entrance is deep enough for those death machines of the American pigs, so why the problem with this poky old garbage scow?'

Angus ignored the insult to his fine ship and answered her without a trace of rancour.

'It is only deep enough at high tide for those big monsters.' he replied, his voice indicating his superior if somewhat deceptive knowledge. 'It is low water just now, and is fairly shallow.'

Being no expert on the Clyde estuary tidal ranges she had to reluctantly accept this plausible argument. After all, she had heard that one of the reasons for siting the base ship there was because the loch could not be entered easily by enemy submarines. Mostly though, the skipper's argument was a pure and simple lie.

Just at the wrong moment though the wheelhouse door swung open and a much recovered Gilly entered, accompanied by his female escort.

'I'm fine now, skipper.' he stated with a slight slur. 'Is there anything you want me to do?'

Before Angus could reply Gilly moved to the bridge front and peered out, gave a slight start, and turned to Angus with a puzzled frown. 'That looks like the lights of the Farnhead in front of us?'

'It must be the whisky in you, laddie!' Angus snapped. 'You've got yourself a wee bit tipsy and are imagining things!'

'But that's Fiddin village up ahead on the port side.' protested the seaman. 'I can even make out the lights of the Londoners Arms!'

'Shut your mouth Gilly!' Angus snapped.

Bella pushed herself forward and stared out at the lights. 'What the hell is going on?' she demanded to know.

'We are going on!' exclaimed Angus with a laugh, and then slammed the telegraph to Full Ahead. 'Give it all you've got, Chief!' he yelled down the voice pipe. 'We will hit the bank anytime now!'

Bella Bolnay finally realised she had been conned. That realisation hit at the same time as the Fiddin ferry hit the shallows between Fiddin Island and the shore. Howling her fury she bowled Gilly and the skipper aside and slammed back the telegraph to Full Astern, but to no avail as the old brass handle snapped cleanly off in her angry and frustrated hand.

McPhee, warned about what was going on, ignored the astern command and the ferry trundled briefly on through mud and clinging weeds before, with a final shudder, churned and slithered to a halt, engines still racing and bow tilting up to the night sky. Only then did McPhee stop his engines.

Angus picked himself out of the tangle of male and female bodies thrown to the front of the wheelhouse by the shock of the abrupt halt, and consulted his large old fashioned pocket watch. 'Ten minutes to high water!' he told them all triumphantly. 'And solidly aground. There will be no more of this carry on tonight, for this boat will not be shifted until we get at least one tug over from Greenock in the morning!'

The voice pipe gave a small satisfied sounding whistle and Angus acknowledged with a brief word before McPhee's voice echoed up.

'I take it, Angus, that we are Finished with Engines for the night?'

The bulk of Fiddin Island deadened the sound of the grounding to those on the Dhu Mohr but all turned and looked back in that direction as a series of small waves curved out from the shallows and lapped against the shore. The slight mist still lingered over the loch but, as the fishing boat turned across the north of the island a faint angular shadow in the shallows could be seen against the lights of Greenock in the distance.

'Hey, maybe the super's right for once!' whispered Jimmy Thomson to Tinkle Bell. 'There's something there in the narrows!'

Smythe Smith could see it as well, a sharp bulk at odds to the feathered trees on either side. His heart leapt in anticipation. 'Hard a Port!' he yelled. 'Stand by for action!'

'It's Starboard, you daft big Sassenach!' retorted Hector. 'And I will not be going right in there! I am not risking my boat!'

'You are under charter to Her Majesty's Customs and Excise!' argued Smythe Smith. 'You'll take this boat where you are told!'

Hector ignored this and kept his heading up Loch Fiddin but at least conceded slightly by reducing speed as he also was intrigued by the obstruction in the Fiddin narrows.

'Now Hector,' Sergeant Donaldson pointed out. 'There is many a time you have cut across the shallows to reach Fiddin before closing time in the Londoners.'

'But that was an emergency!' exclaimed Hector.

'This is a real emergency!' howled Smythe Smith. 'Get this boat turned round or I will have Sergeant Donaldson arrest you for obstructing justice!'

Hector glowered at the customs super, but didn't want to put his cousin Donald in an awkward position. 'Och, all right! But it will be costing you double to hire my boat after this. I will be wanting some of that dangerous money stuff!'

He spun the wheel round to Starboard and the boat

heeled over nearly tipping Smythe Smith out of the open wheelhouse door, then straightened it up and headed through the darkness towards the east side of the island.

'I hope old Hector knows what he's doing' whispered Jimmy Thomson anxiously. 'I'm not the world's best swimmer.'

'Don't worry about it' Tinkle whispered back. 'Drunk, blindfolded and in thick fog he could find his way about here. He knows every shoal and rock in the estuary by its first name. The old phony is only objecting like that to bump up his charter price!'

Commander Lewis Clarke, hair blowing in the wind caused by the high speed, shouted down from the flying bridge of the Chris Craft to his two subordinates below.

'Maitland, come up and take the con and head straight for the lights of that freighter. Padowski, find the switch for the navigation lights. We're going for these commies in the dark and we ain't gonna give them any warnings!'

The two sailors looked at each other and shrugged, but did as they were told. You did not disobey a full blown commander in the US Navy even if you did think he was nuts! Maitland took the con and the speeding craft roared towards the east channel.

'You know the loch well, Commander?' asked the anxious Maitland Jnr. 'I mean, I hope there are no big toothed rocks up ahead for I sure don't fancy taking a dip in the loch tonight.'

'No problem!' assured Clarke. 'There's nothing between us and that ship but a slightly shallower bit and we'll cross that no bother at this state of the tide'

He turned to Padowski just as the navigation lights clicked off. 'You see a switch there for a searchlight?'

'Sure thing, sir I'm ready when you are.'

'Okay then. They are out in that loch somewhere! When

I give the word, get the commie S.O.B's right in the spotlight! They try anything and I'll blast them with this old cannon of mines!' He waved his vintage revolver in the air. 'Tonight's the night that we fix these commies for once and for all!'

The two sailors looked at each other in horror, and then silently shook their heads. He was a commander, but he was most definitely nuts!

Aboard the Dhu Mohr, Smythe Smith pointed frantically down the narrows. 'Donaldson, I saw lights for a moment but they've doused them so they can sneak past! Head straight that way!' He turned to the other two customs men. 'Get that portable floodlight ready and get up the top of the wheelhouse. When I shout, blind the villains!'

Bella Bolnay strode about the ferry ranting and raving in her fury, but knowing she could do nothing now that wouldn't make the situation even worse. She glowered up to the darkened corner of the bridge where Angus Kerr stood, quietly puffing away on his pipe and relishing his triumph. A harassed looking McPhee joined him there a few moments later waving his hands in disgust. 'Damn switchboard blew when we grounded, Angus.' he said regretfully. 'No chance of getting lights on tonight, let alone anything else. There is pipes and valves and fuse boxes and switches knocked to hell and gone and lying about hanging from wires, and me with only one wee torch to find my way about the engine room.'

'Now don't you be worrying about a thing, Willie' assured the skipper. 'We will be getting Lloyds and a tug and all the repair men you need, across from Greenock in the morning. A wee bit of payback for all that fancy insurance I have been paying all these years.'

McPhee nodded reluctantly. 'Ah well, I suppose we are

safe enough sitting here on top of the bank, but I would like to have seen into the double bottoms to see if there is any hull damage, but I can't see a thing down that pit

'It's a tough old boat, McPhee, not like these tin boxes they make these days. Now the water will be low enough around dawn to walk round outside on the bank to have a look, and for sure somebody ashore will be calling our stranding in. No doubt there will be all sorts of experts turning up to have a poke as well.' He raised his voice to ensure the now subdued Mothers against Polaris could hear as well. 'And no doubt the local police and maybe the American Navy will be along as well to sort that lot out!'

It was merely a threat except for the likelihood of somebody calling it in. Fiddin was not far and he wouldn't be surprised if already somebody was coming along to investigate. Then the sound of boat engines rising to a noisy crescendo made it more a prediction.

'Now who would that be, running about the loch at this time of night?' the skipper asked.

'Two boats by the sound of it.' said McPhee, his engineer's ear picking out the distinctive sounds of two very different engines. 'And damn close at that!'

'Now!' shouted Smythe Smith to his portable searchlight wielders

'Now!' echoed Lewis Clarke in triumphant anticipation.

Two blinding lights shot across the shallows from either end, wavering for a moment before meeting in a conflicting light surge beneath wheel house of the little ferry then focussing directly on the opposing and rapidly approaching boats.

Maitland Jnr. threw his hands over his eyes. 'I can't see!' he yelled, and ducked down instinctively.

The Chris Craft roared on.

Hector Donaldson screwed his eyes tight shut. 'What

the hell?' he shouted, unheard by the customs men hanging off the top of the wheelhouse who were also completely blinded.

The Dhu Mohr held her course though.

The Chris Craft struck the lowered after ramp of the ferry, reared into the air on her sharp bow, then continued on crashing down and sliding along the chequered steel deck ripping big lumps out of its fibre glass hull. Lewis Clarke, for once in his life, was lucky. Thrown flat by the shock of the collision, he avoided decapitation as the flimsy flying bridge was sliced off by the steel girder underside of the ferry wheelhouse. As the Chris Craft jammed between there and the deck, it came to a crunching stop with half the below the waterline of the hull lying about in splinters and the flying bridge little but a torn up mangled mess.

The remains stopped just short of a screaming mass of Mothers against Polaris who had been huddled close to the side cabins and shelter and protected slightly from the cold by the raised forward ramp.

Then the Dhu More hit the forward ramp and many were catapulted along the ferry deck as it was jerked astern with a crashing medley of smashing wood and buckling steel.

The two young customs men precariously balanced on the fishing boat wheelhouse had no chance of holding on and were catapulted over the front of the boat and the ferry ramp, luckily finding a soft landing among the much abused women huddled on the ferry deck. Inside all were thrown forward, a fair weight, and the sixty plus years of rot that had severely weakened the joint where the fishing boat wheelhouse met the deck, parted suddenly, and the wheelhouse ripped forward taking with it Hector, Donald and Smythe Smith. It hit the top of the ramp, toppled over slowly, and landed upside down with a crash, just behind the ramp, the three inside struggling to free themselves.

Chaos reigned on the pitch black deck as various groups tried to free themselves from the wreckage, the only lights being a couple of small torches, then from the depths of the loch appeared a strange shape, dark and glistening, shedding water from its sleek sides, two big glowing eyes staring out. A strange whine came from its bowels and two large gleaming appendages turned and stared at the melee on the ferry deck.

'It is the monster itself!' exclaimed Hector as he was helped up from the wheelhouse wreckage.

'It's damn commie spies!' contradicted Lewis Clarke, still obsessed with an imagined threat.

'Bloody drug smugglers!' roared Smythe Smith, whose brain, even after upending, was still totally one track.

Sergeant Donaldson shook crumbled glass from his hair and stared out and nearly laughed. 'Nothing at all like that! It is only the Taff twins from the Farnhead, and their wee homemade submarine!'

The wet suited twins played there powerful underwater lights on the chaos aboard the ferry and shook their heads in unison. 'Looks like they have had a fairly interesting night.' said Michael David.

'And they didn't even invite us to join the party!' added David Michael.

As the lights played along the ferry side Bella Bolnay leant over and looked at the water below. 'We're afloat again!' she cried, a hint of possibility in her voice. Bella was never one to give up.

'I do not think it matters too much if that bump did knock us off the bank.' said Angus, indicating the shambles on the deck. 'We are not going anywhere.'

'It matters a great deal!' shouted McPhee as he swung out the engine door after a quick look down below. 'There's water coming in at the bow where that boat hit, and we're sinking fast!'

'And my wee boat is sinking as well!' Hector groaned ruefully as he looked over the bow ramp. 'Both halves of it!'

'And I guess I am well and truly sunk!' moaned Lewis Clarke, surveying the devastating wreckage of his captain's pride and joy.

'Ah well, I will just be nipping down below for the ferry insurance policy.' said an unperturbed Angus Kerr. 'In the meantime, Gilly, give the chief a hand as I we might as well break out those inflatable life rafts of ours, though I doubt if it will sink far enough onto the bank here to even cover the deck. Still, better safe than sorry, so we will take to the boats anyway.'

Gilly raised his eyebrows in surprise at the captain's cool appraisal of things, and then saw a dark glower move over his face. 'And I suppose, much as I regret it, I expect I had better be letting those so called women go first!'

EPILOGUE

A small launch lay in the dark glass-like waters of Loch, Fiddin and, mirrored in those waters, a solitary figure sat reeling in his fishing line, a gleaming arm length fish twisting on the hook. Colin Cameron was still enjoying the excellent fishing and particularly so, as this was his last morning before going home on a month's leave. His relief, Patrick O'Hagan, would arrive later that day and the twins would have to suffer their arch enemy for a week before they too would go on leave from the Farnhead. Much as he enjoyed the fishing here, Colin would be glad to get back to his family. Besides, he was quite sure he had found and drunk the last bottle of O'Hagan's hidden rum supply!

A few hundred yards away a small trail of bubbles broke the surface marking the progress of the twin's submersible as the continued their determined search for Prince Charlie's treasure. Colin smiled wryly. Believing in the treasure was almost as futile as believing in the Fiddin Monster! But it kept them occupied and did no harm during what was really a boring job.

Down at the loch entrance a salvage barge was removing the last wreckage of the triple collisions of the previous week. At high water the old ferry still remained visible but divers had soon ascertained that the damage to it, combined with its age, and the other craft made them all total write offs. It only remained to clear the shallow Fiddin Island channel and the whole event would be history, though by mutual agreement of all the parties involved, largely unwritten history.

Luckily little damage had been done to the participants in that night's debacle. A few scratches and bruises, a lot of wounded pride, and several badly dented egos. Though for some, it had its positively advantageous side.

Hector, after much humming and hawing, had accepted a recently confiscated, and much newer, fishing boat from a severely embarrassed Customs and Excise department. They liked to cover their mistakes and had also removed Hector's old adversary from the scene, sending Smythe Smith off to the mountains of Wales to check on wholly unsubstantiated rumours of illegal distilling in the area. Hopefully all he would find to annoy there would be a few black faced sheep.

The rest of the Customs team had been returned to normal duties, though Sergeant Donaldson had been given the unenviable task of providing part of the permanent police presence at the gates of the American landing dock.

That was hardly likely to cause him a lot of harassment though in the few months till his retirement as most of the Mothers against Polaris had decided the Scottish lochs were not for them, and had slipped away to greener and more common pastures in the south. Deciding that discretion was the order of the day, their disgraced leader, the now disillusioned Bella Bolnay, had swiftly departed the country and rumour had it that she intended to head for the Himalayas to protest about nuclear fall-out there.

Commander Lewis Clarke had also been swiftly removed to other parts, promoted sideways to head his own small attachment guarding a seldom used emergency airfield in an isolated part of the South Pacific. This was as far from any communist influences as the U.S. Navy could find. A significant part of his detachment consisted of Maitland Jnr. and Padowski. The latter, having escaped the clutches of a broken hearted Hot Helen, was looking forward to the fabled hula girls of the region, but was soon disappointed. They had all long since left for California and the chance of Hollywood stardom.

The insurance company, prodded by HM Customs and a few politicians, agreed to pay for a new ferry, or at least a low mileage second hand one, and Angus and McPhee would continue to ply their trade, though it was said that Gilly had sworn never to set foot on a ship again, and had applied for a job as a fire tower warden with the Forestry Commission. As part of the agreement to quietly cover up the involvement of certain female friends of the local left leaning council, Angus had magnanimously accepted a small increase in the annual ferry subsidy, which would give him and McPhee a few extra drams before dinner every night. And maybe a few after as well.

All in all, a nice tidy bunch of packages and all was peaceful again on Loch Fiddin.

More bubbles erupted from the loch, then suddenly a black rubber sleeved arm shot aloft bearing a gleaming golden sword, a sheathed Excalibur, glinting untarnished by its two centuries or so immersion in the depths. The home made submarine surfaced in a welter of foam and the excited twins whipped off their face masks.

'We've found it! We've found it!' they cried in chorus.

'Oh no!' exclaimed Colin, visions of a hundred treasure hunting boats roaring about the previously quiet waters. 'The buggars will ruin the fishing!'

THE END

Other books by Jack Kirk available on Amazon Books.
All except "Malky Machinery Colouring Book" available on Kindle.

Dark Immortal – Fiction - Adventure and crime. 1st of Immortal series.

Red Immortal – Fiction - Adventure and crime. 2nd of Immortal series.

Village of Fear - Fiction- Adventure & Crime- Set in Philadelphia present day.

A Flood of Spears- Fiction-Adventure with a magic touch. Set in a fictitious 11th century Britain with a difference. First of Fire Mountains series.

A Torrent of Ships- Fiction-Adventure with a magic touch. Set in a fictitious 11th century Britain with a difference. Second of Fire Mountains series. (2 books)

Defend or Die – Science Fiction- An alien invasion of Earth in the present day.
1st in Aakron Annihilation series (3 books)

Defy and Deny – Science Fiction- An alien invasion of Earth in the present day.
2nd in Aakron Annihilation series (3 books)

Attack and Annihilate - Science Fiction- An alien invasion of Earth in the present day. 3rd in Aakron Annihilation series (3 books)

A Basket of Life and Death- Fiction. Short stories. With a few Illustrations.

Imagination- Fiction. Poetry & Clipart-Illustrated.

Voyages 1- Fact- The author's life in the British Merchant Navy as an Engineer. Years 1968 to 1991. (2 books)

Voyages 2- Fact- The author's life in the British Merchant Navy as an Engineer. Years 1991 to 2006. (2 books)

Digital Duntocher- Fact- An Illustrated view of the small Village of Duntocher, Scotland, showing typical and prominent buildings in and around it.

The Malevolent Machinery- Illustrated Humour-The authors take on the danger from machinery

Malky Machinery Colouring Book- Colouring book for Adults and children

The Bankie Booze Trail- Humorous illustrated guide to Clydebank pubs.

Armageddon City- Science fiction, first of series on a world almost destroyed.

Digital Drinking-fact- the author's personal guide to world pubs- illustrated.

Printed in Great Britain
by Amazon